Things were not right in Martin Leonard's room; I could feel it in the air again. It was not just that someone had been there who didn't belong. There was a smell in the air that I had become quite familiar with over the years.

The smell of death.

I found him in the bathroom, stuffed into the tub. The blood led in dry tracks to the drain, dark brown and crusted. He'd been killed sometime the night before, shot in the head.

In my effort to figure out who would want Leonard dead, I wondered if the Russians somehow decided that he was a danger? What if they hadn't fingered me as an American agent, but Martin Leonard instead?

That being the case, it could very well have been me lying in the bathtub with a bullet through my head.

And if the Russians realized their mistake, I could very well be next . . .

NICK CARTER IS IT!

"Nick Carter out-Bonds James Bond."
—*Buffalo Evening News*

"Nick Carter is America's #1 espionage agent."
—*Variety*

"Nick Carter is razor-sharp suspense."
—*King Features*

"Nick Carter is extraordinarily big."
—*Bestsellers*

"Nick Carter has attracted an army of addicted readers . . . the books are fast, have plenty of action and just the right degree of sex . . . Nick Carter is the American James Bond, suave, sophisticated, a killer with both the ladies and the enemy."
—*The New York Times*

Dedicated to the men of the
Secret Services of the
United States of America

A Killmaster Spy Chiller

NICK CARTER

CHESSMASTER

CHARTER
NEW YORK

A Division of Charter Communications Inc.
A GROSSET & DUNLAP COMPANY
51 Madison Avenue
New York, New York 10010

CHESSMASTER
Copyright © 1982 by The Condé Nast Publications, Inc.
All rights reserved. No part of this book may be reproduced in
any form or by any means except for the inclusion of brief
quotations in a review, without permission in writing from the
publisher.

All characters in this book are fictitious. Any resemblance to
actual persons living or dead, is purely coincidental.

"Nick Carter" is a registered trademark of The Condé Nast
Publications, Inc. registered in the United States Patent Office.

An Ace Charter Original.

First Ace Charter Printing January 1982
Published simultaneously in Canada
Manufactured in the United States of America

2 4 6 8 0 9 7 5 3 1

CHESSMASTER

ONE

I hadn't done too badly, considering I had spent most of my life as a Killmaster. In fact, up until about a month ago, I only had general knowledge of the game. Nick Carter, Chessmaster. I couldn't get used to that—and probably never would.

Anyway, here I was competing against some of the finest players in the world in Atlantic City, and I was on the verge of a victory that would put me right in the finals. Who would have thought when Hawk first approached me a month ago that I would have come this far?

"How well do you know the game of chess?" my boss, David Hawk asked me.

"I have a working knowledge," I admitted, puzzled at the question. David Hawk didn't usually make a habit of discussing games or sports with his operatives.

"I enjoy the game," I had commented, "but I'm hardly an expert at it."

"Well, as of now, you have just under a month to become just that—an expert," he had informed me.

"What are you talking about, sir?"

"I'll explain further, N3, but first does the name Alexi Belnikov mean anything to you?"

It might not have struck a cord so quickly had we not

just been talking about chess, but I put two and two together and came up with Belnikov, the Soviet Chessmaster.

"He's the new Soviet champion, isn't he?" I asked.

"Precisely. He wants to defect."

I raised my eyebrows in surprise.

Hawk fixed me with his steely gray eyes and launched into his explanation. "As their champion, Belnikov is a privileged citizen of the Soviet Union, and as such is privy to information he would otherwise not have access to. He offers us this information, which he assures us will help the United States stay more than one step ahead of the Soviets, as an act of good faith. After that we must help him to escape."

"Would he really have access to information that damaging to the Russians?" I asked. "I mean, he is just a chess player."

"We won't really know that, N3, until he gives it to us."

"I suppose not," I relented.

"In any case, his defection would be a coup. So we'll play it his way—for now."

"Which means that I have to learn how to play chess competitively, against some of the finest players in the world, in under a month," I summed up.

"A month from now there is a national tournament being played in Atlantic City," Hawk said. "If you compete and do well enough, you will be eligible to compete in the world tournament in Switzerland the following week."

"How do you propose to get me into shape in time for the tournament?" I asked.

"Evan Clarke. Clarke was a world champion ten or twelve years ago. He retired from competition after he lost his championship, but he has agreed to tutor you in the finer points of chess strategy."

"How long does it generally take someone to become

a world-class player?" I asked, having some doubts about the entire plan.

"That doesn't matter, N3," he told me. "You have twenty-nine days in which to do it, and I have every confidence—"

"Thank you, sir," I said over-confidently, cutting him off.

"—in Evan Clarke," Hawk finished his sentence.

"Oh."

I had no sooner walked into his house in New Milford, Connecticut and removed my coat when he had me seated across the board from him. Evan Clarke was a pleasant looking, short, rotund man in his early sixties who, after playing two games with me, announced that I obviously had no concept of defense and absolutely no end game.

"How am I otherwise?" I asked.

"Terrible—but we can fix that. You are very offense minded, and consequently you leave yourself wide open on defense."

"So that means that if my offense fails, if I make a mistake, I'm open to almost any kind of attack from my opponent," I remarked, trying to sound as if I weren't totally hopeless.

He shook his head. "You make the same mistake most young chess players do, Mr. Carter. The idea in chess is not to avoid mistakes, that's next to impossible. The idea is to make the next-to-last mistake. The man who does that is a winning chess player."

He set the chess pieces up again, but not for another game. Once they were lined up, he rose from his chair.

"Chess is a sport," he told me, "and you will train as any other athlete does. You will obey me implicitly. If you do, I guarantee that you will be able to play a decent, competitive game of chess."

"And win?"

He stared balefully at me over his eyeglasses and said, "That, young fellow, was not part of the deal." He took a pipe down from the mantlepiece and began packing it. "I guaranteed that I would teach you enough about chess strategy so that you would be able to play competitively on a high level. As far as winning goes, that's up to you."

"How's that?"

He held a pipe lighter to the bowl of his pipe and created clouds of smoke until he had it going to his satisfaction.

"As with any great athlete, the most important thing is his attitude, his desire to win. If you want to win bad enough, and you have the tools, then you can win. I will supply the tools, but you must supply the desire. Understand?"

"Perfectly."

"Very well then, let's get started."

For the next twenty-seven days I did nothing but read books, listen to him lecture, review classic matches and play chess.

After fifteen days, I had lost two hundred games in a row. On day sixteen, I stalemated him, which in chess language means that we played to a tie.

He sat, frowning at the board. "That shouldn't have happened," he remarked, puzzled.

"But it did," I told him. "It happened in 1918, 1943 and, most recently, in 1967—and now it's happened again tonight," I explained.

"You remembered this situation from classic matches played on those dates?" he asked, surprised.

"I have an excellent memory," I told him.

"So I see," he murmured, still staring at the board.

"Can I go to sleep now?" I asked, stretching.

"Yes, yes, go to sleep. I want to study this."

I left him staring at the board and retired for the night, feeling very smug and self-satisfied.

By day twenty-five I wasn't feeling so smug. I hadn't even come close to winning a game since the stalemate.

"Frustrated?" he asked.

"Thoroughly," I admitted.

"You don't want it bad enough," he told me. "You think about that tonight."

I thought about it, and the following day, on day twenty-six, I stalemated him again.

"Well played," he told me, which was the first time he'd ever complimented me.

"Thanks."

On the twenty-eighth day I won a game.

On the final day, we played eight games and I won two, and stalemated a third.

"You're a quick study, Nick," he told me after the final game, "and you're ready."

So here I was, zeroed in on my opponent's king in my semi-final match of the Atlantic City chess tournament that one month ago I didn't even know about.

I was six moves away from checkmating my opponent.

"Well played," my opponent told me.

"Thank you."

"I resign," Nikki Barnes announced, then leaned across the board and put her beautiful face close to mine and said, "Now let's go to your room and play a different kind of game."

TWO

Nikki Barnes was one of three women entered in the Atlantic City competition. She was tall, brunette and wonderfully constructed. She looked quite young, yet she exhibited an air of mature sophistication. She had full, large breasts, ample hips and thighs, and a behind that she carried very well. Her mouth was full and wide, and her eyes were pale, sometimes seeming green, sometimes gray.

She was also a very good chess player.

I had met her on my first day in Atlantic City, as all of the players had gathered for the draw.

"Those green eyes could easily make a man forget why he's here," I told her.

She favored me with a wide, gorgeous smile. "Who do I have to thank for that charming, bullshit remark?" she asked, raising her eyebrows.

"Nicholas Crane. And I'm sincere. I hope to convince you of that over dinner this evening."

She thought it over for a moment, then nodded as if she'd made her decision. "Room 1214," she told me. "Would eight be too late?"

"Eight would be perfect. Knowing your name would be extremely helpful, too."

"I'm sure it would," she answered. "I'm Nikki Barnes, and I believe in omens."

"Which means?"

She stepped forward and made chest-to-chest contact. "The similarity in our names. I believe it's an omen, Nick, and perhaps tonight we'll find out if it's a positive one, or a negative one."

"Well, I believe in omens too, Nikki—but only the positive kind."

"See you at eight," she promised, and was gone.

There were no matches the first day, so I tried out the casino for awhile, without much success. Evan Clarke's philosophy had proven true even there. My mind was not on gambling, and my desire was most certainly somewhere else.

Eight couldn't come soon enough for me and when it did I was knocking on her door. She opened it and I caught my breath.

She wore a sheer blue gown without a bra, and the nipples of her large breasts were very much in evidence.

"Beautiful," I said, truthfully and almost reverently.

She took both of my hands and drew me into the room. I shut the door behind me and asked her where she wanted to go for dinner.

"I made a decision while I was dressing," she informed me.

"And what was that?"

"I decided that I would take a page out of your book."

"Which page?"

"The one about only believing in good omens," she explained.

"Which means what?"

"Which means," she continued, stepped up close, "maybe we'll go to dinner later."

She molded her body against mine, put her arms around my neck and crushed her mouth to mine. I cupped the cheeks of her beautiful behind and pulled her close, until we were grinding our pelvises together.

She broke the embrace and walked into the next room. I counted to ten and then followed, loosening my tie. I found her standing naked next to the turned-down bed.

Her body was perfect. Her breasts were tipped with large, copper-colored nipples which were now swollen with passion. Her belly wasn't flat, but rounded slightly, the perfect launching pad for the rocket that was now swollen between my legs.

She came to me and began to remove my clothing. I caressed her firm, smooth breasts, cupping their roundness, flicking the nipples with my thumbs and forefingers until she fell to her knees, taking them from my reach.

She removed the remainder of my clothing and took the length of me into her mouth. When I couldn't take much more of that she got back to her feet and drew me with her to the bed. She lay down and pulled me down on top of her. Her flesh was burning hot, and her hands were on my manhood, pulling it toward her.

"Now, Nick, now, I need you inside of me now," she moaned, pulling insistently.

As hot as her flesh was, inside she was like an inferno. I slid in very slowly, until the full length of me was surrounded by her. Nikki's hips were up off the bed as she tried to pull me deeper still. I withdrew as slowly as I had entered, then suddenly rammed myself back in as hard as I could.

She screamed, wrapped her legs around me and held on tightly. I grasped the cheeks of her behind firmly and drove myself as fast as possible. She moaned loudly into my ear, the breath being crushed from her lungs.

"Nick, Nick, Nick . . ." she chanted repeatedly. I knew she was ready as her cries increased in tempo. Then I was ready too, and we exploded together.

As she attempted to get her breath back I began nibbling on her nipples. Then I raised myself above her and she smiled a smile that lit up her entire face.

I smiled back at her, kissed her, placed my mouth next to her right ear and whispered, "That's check and mate."

She snaked her hand between us, took hold of me firmly and growled, "Best two out of three."

THREE

We had breakfast together in her room, then spent the morning on the beach. We each had a match after lunch, so we separated upon leaving the beach, agreeing to meet later for dinner.

I lost my match to a fellow named Martin Leonard. He was about thirty-eight, tall, slim, graying slightly at the temples. His game was conservative, and that part of it seemed to carry over into his personality and dress. He offered to buy me a drink, and I took him up on it.

"You play well," he told me while we waited for our drinks.

"Not well enough, I guess," I answered.

"No, quite the contrary," he insisted. "You took a risk toward the end and it backfired. If it had worked, you would have won."

"The next to last mistake," I said, only half aloud.

"What was that?"

"Oh, nothing. Just something somebody told me once," I assured him. "It wasn't important."

Our drinks came and he finished his right off, then ordered another. "I haven't seen you around before, Nick," he said between gulps.

"Well, I've never seen you before, either," I answered, hoping he wasn't going to get too nosy.

"I keep pretty good track of the better players, the up-and-coming players," he told me. "You're just short of one, and too old for the other, so—"

I interrupted him before he could go any further. "Then that might explain why you don't remember me," I told him. I gave my watch a quick check and then said, "Excuse me, I have to meet someone."

He held his drink up to me and said, "Don't feel bad about losing to me. I'm going to win this tournament."

"Good luck," I told him, and left the bar.

Hawk had made sure that I was filled in on most of the players who would be competing at this Atlantic City tournament. The file on Nikki Barnes revealed nothing of interest, but the one on Martin Leonard indicated that he was apparently the type of player who was always referred to as having "great potential," but had never quite been able to fulfill it. He won a tournament now and then, but had been unable to win with any consistancy over the past twelve years. He was now approaching forty and he wasn't "the kid" anymore. He was also known to hit the bottle heavily, but only after a match. He'd probably be there at the bar for quite a while.

I decided to pass up the casino and go for a walk.

The competition was still going on as I strolled the boardwalk, as my match had been one of the earliest scheduled ones. The beach was sparsely inhabited, and I was virtually alone on the boardwalk. Early diners were inside, stuffing themselves in anticipation of a big night at the tables.

I don't necessarily believe in ESP, but I do believe in a strong sense of survival. Something made me turn around and look behind me when I did, and that something saved my life.

He had probably climbed up over the side of the boardwalk from the beach, because had he approached me from further back, or had he followed me, I would have noticed earlier. As I turned, he was coming at me with a long knife—like a hunting blade—and he was preparing to rearrange my innards. When he saw me turn he stopped and began to slowly approach me, holding the knife out in front of him. He thought I was unarmed until he saw Hugo pop into my hand.

Killing an unarmed man was one thing, but facing a man with a knife didn't seem to sit well with him. He flicked his eyes left and right, looking for an out, and decided to go the way he came. He dashed to the right, leaped the rail and dropped to the beach below. I made my decision and went over the rail to my right. Sure enough, I caught him cutting underneath.

Now we were in the sand and we both still had our knives out. This was also a different story. First he had been prepared to kill an unarmed man, then he had decided to run. Now, in order to get away, he had to fight. I wanted him alive, but it's hard to disarm a man who's looking to kill you. Usually, you look to kill him first.

"We can avoid this, friend," I told him. "I just want to know who sent you, and why. How about it?"

He was a beach-boy type—tall, lots of dark hair, large shoulders and hands—but he was more used to posing than he was to fighting.

Then again, he must have had a reason for deciding to give it a try. Maybe because he was bigger than I was, and his knife was bigger than mine. Whatever the reason, he came at me with that big hunting knife stuck out in front of him like some kind of a unicorn. I could have sidestepped him and cut him open with Hugo, but I wanted him alive. I went down to one knee and allowed the hand holding the knife to pass over my right shoulder. Then I picked him up and dumped him over my back. As he fell I turned quickly to be ready for him if and when he got up. What I hadn't realized was that we were so close to one of the pilings. He had struck the piling wrong, and I knew he wasn't going to be getting up. His neck was broken.

FOUR

My assignment was hardly even underway and it appeared as if I was blown already.

I worked my way back to the hotel beneath the boardwalk, hoping that no one had witnessed the action of moments ago. On my way back to my room I passed the bar and saw Martin Leonard just where I left him. Up in my room I washed my hands and face, then settled down to go over the problem in my mind.

Somebody had sent the man to kill me, because it was obvious to me that it wasn't his own idea. The question was this: did this attempt on my life have something to do with my present assignment, or was it something else entirely? I had not seen any familiar faces around, but that didn't necessarily mean that there wasn't someone around who might have recognized me.

Either way I was going to have to keep my guard up, both here in Atlantic City and in Switzerland at the World Competition.

I decided to go back down to the competition. When the body under the boardwalk was discovered, I wanted to be around a crowd of people.

I got down in time to watch Nikki's match. About halfway through, with her fighting a piece down, a rumble began to ripple through the room, and I knew that the body had been discovered. I kept my attention on the game as Nikki did some excellent maneuvering and, still a piece down, was able to defeat her opponent who, after the game, complained that the crowd had disturbed his concentration.

"Congratulations," I told Nikki.

"Thanks. How'd you do?"

"Not as well as you, I'm afraid."

"I'm sorry. What was that hubbub through the crowd about?" she asked.

"Beats me. How about a drink to celebrate your victory?"

"Sounds good to me. Were you here for most of it?"

"I sure was. You played brilliantly toward the end."

"I know. I got careless early and lost a piece, but I play better when I'm down a piece or two."

We went into the bar arm and arm, and there was a small crowd around the door that led out to the beach and the boardwalk. I noticed some uniformed police among them.

"I wonder what that's all about?" Nikki asked.

"My guess is we'll find out soon enough. Whatever it is, it looks big enough so that it will get around."

"I guess you're right."

We took a table and ordered our drinks.

"Here's to Switzerland," I told her. Neither of us would win this particular competition, but it was quite possible that we had each acquitted ourselves well enough to go to the Swiss competition.

"I'll drink to that. With both of us there, it could turn out to be a very enjoyable trip," she added.

We ordered a second round and when the waiter brought the drinks, Nikki's curiousity got the better of her. "What's all the commotion about?" she asked him.

"Some swimmers found a body underneath the boardwalk," he told her.

"That's terrible. Who was he?"

"One of the lifeguards down the beach, I hear."

"What happened to him?"

"Somebody said he had a broken neck, but I don't know for sure."

She thanked him, then with her chin in her hand, pondered out loud, "I wonder what happened out there?"

"We can read the papers tomorrow, but we'll probably never know what really happened," I told her.

"I guess you're right."

She dropped the subject, and I was glad she did. I wondered if any of the hotel employees would remember me going out onto the boardwalk, or coming back in shortly thereafter. They would all surely be questioned about what guests had gone out on or come off of the boardwalk between certain hours. I had struck up a conversation with a few of the others who were watching Nikki's match, and I was hoping that they would be a little fuzzy on just what time it was when they saw me. I had to be ready with answers, just in case the local police came to me with questions.

Actually, we were stopped on our way out of the bar by a uniformed police officer who asked me if I was Nicholas Crane.

"Yes, I am."

"Would you come with me, sir?" he asked.

"What for?"

"Lieutenant Beck would like to ask you a few questions, sir."

"About what?" I asked.

He was a young guy, not yet thirty, but he had poise and would not allow me to push him any further.

"Sir, if you would accompany me, I'm sure the lieutenant could answer all of your questions to your satisfaction," he suggested.

I decided to go along.

"Meet you upstairs?" I asked Nikki.

"No way. I'm going with you. This may be the only

way I'll find out what really happened out there."

Obviously, she was sure that the body under the boardwalk was what the police wanted to question me about. I had hoped to play dumb with them, but she had killed that strategy for me pretty well with her last remarks.

"Do you think that's what this is about?" I asked as we followed the young officer.

"Why else would the police want to talk to you?" she asked, then added, "I wonder what makes them think you know anything?"

"I guess we'll find out from Lieutenant Beck."

The lieutenant had apparently set himself up in the manager's office. The officer brought us in and introduced me to the lieutenant.

Beck was a big man in his mid-forties, with salt-and-pepper hair, a sharp nose and an overall non-coplike face. He looked like a good-humored man, but right now he was frowning.

"Mr. Crane, thank you for coming," he told me after the introduction.

"Happy to cooperate, lieutenant," I told him. "This is my friend—and competitor—Miss Barnes."

"Lieutenant," she said.

"Have a seat please, Miss Barnes. I won't detain you and Mr. Crane very long."

Nikki sat on a couch by the wall, while I took the chair that had been set out for me, right in front of the manager's desk. Behind the desk sat the good lieutenant.

"Mr. Crane, I understand that you went for a walk on the boardwalk this afternoon."

"Is there a law against that?" I asked.

"No, but there's a law against leaving dead bodies lying around underneath the boardwalk," he shot back.

I waited a couple of beats—for effect—then asked, "Should I have a lawyer?"

"Only if you've got something to hide?"

"Am I under arrest?"

"Nope."

"Am I under suspicion for something?"

"You're getting warm."

"Can we cut the crap and get to it?"

"Okay." He shook a cigarette out of a pack of Camels and lit one up. When he had a fair smokescreen built up he said, "We found a body underneath the walk. I'm supposed to find out how and why. To do that I have to ask questions."

"And get answers," I added.

"True. Am I going to get any?"

"Why not? Shoot."

"You go for a walk on the boardwalk?"

"Everyday that I've been here."

"Today?"

I made a show of thinking about it. "Yeah, I think I was on the boardwalk sometime today."

"What time might that have been?" he asked.

I looked at the ceiling, as if it were a gyp sheet with the answers on it. "Uh, I don't really remember."

"Could it have been around four o'clock?"

"No."

Beck looked past me, because I wasn't the one who had spoken. He looked at Nikki and said, "Pardon me?"

"It couldn't have been at four," she told him.

"And how would you know that, Miss Barnes?"

"Because he was in the ballroom watching my chess match at four o'clock," she told him. "And he was there for the entire contest."

Beck leaned forward and crushed out his cigarette.

"You sure about that?" he asked.

"I'm sure," she told him.

"It can be checked," he said, looking at me.

"So, check it," I told him.

He looked at both of us, shook out another Camel

and lit it. Seemed like he couldn't think unless his head was in a cloud of thick smoke. "You can go," he said, finally.

FIVE

After the Atlantic City tournament—which Martin Leonard blew by drinking all night and then trying to play his early morning final match with a hangover—Nikki and I split up at the airport, saying goodbye until Switzerland. I went back to Washington and a meeting with Hawk.

After I told him about the incident on the boardwalk he said, "I'll get in touch with the Jersey Police and see what I can find out about the victim. How did you do in the tournament, by the way?" he asked.

"I didn't win, but I'll be going to Switzerland."

"Evan Clarke will be happy to hear that, I'm sure," he told me.

"Maybe he'll even be surprised," I suggested.

"I think not. He told me that if you devoted your time solely to chess, you'd be a master in record time."

"Mmm, too bad I haven't the time," I told him. Several other things came to mind that I'd rather devote my time to.

"Indeed." He opened a drawer and took out a brown envelope. Handing it across to me he said, "Here is your ticket to Switzerland. The plane leaves tomorrow evening, the competition starts the following day."

I took the envelope and tucked it away in my inner

jacket pocket. "I think I'll get some dinner," I told him, rising, "and then go downstairs to the range."

"It will be closed that late," he reminded me.

"That's okay," I assured him. "I'll get a key before I leave for dinner. I'll return it in the morning."

"Keep in touch with me, N3. I want to know how everything is progressing. Remember, we want Belnikov."

"I'll remember, sir. Good night."

I had a quick dinner alone, then went home and changed my clothes. I put on jeans, a sweatshirt and a nylon windbreaker; beneath the windbreaker I tucked Wilhelmina. I figured plunking a few man-sized targets would relax me, so I intended to give it about a half hour's worth, then go home, read a book and hit the sack.

I showed my pass to the guard at the door of the building AXE used in Washington. He let me pass and I made my way down to the basement. I used a small key to open an otherwise impossible to open large metal door.

Inside I hit the main switch and bathed the room in artificial daylight. I could also hit some switches and simulate almost any kind of lighting at all: dawn, dusk, whatever.

It was almost like an arcade shooting gallery. I hit the automatic switch and the targets began to move by themselves. I began to pick them off fairly easily, and got bored quickly. I turned to accelerate the targets with the flick of another switch, when the lights went out.

That wasn't supposed to happen, not if I was alone down there.

Which meant I wasn't alone.

I went down into a crouch and slipped another clip into Wilhelmina as quietly as possible. The only way I could play it was to stay where I was and wait. Wait for whoever else was down there to come at me. I may or may not have had an edge on him. I knew the setup down there, but I didn't know if he knew. The odds were that if he was able to get into the room and cut the lights, then he did know his way around.

He'd been down there before.

Which meant that we had a leak in AXE.

I stayed still as long as I possibly could, but when my knees began to ache I had to shift. I did it as quietly as I could, but to me my feet scraping the floor sounded like a hell of a racket. Just in case he heard it, I shifted a few feet to my right, down one of the target chutes.

I sat down on the floor, removed my shoes and then moved up into a crouch again. Since I had the shoes in my hand I decided to use them. I threw them into the air and they landed two or three target chutes down. He was good enough not to panic, overreact and maybe throw a shot in the direction of the shoes. I only hoped that the noise, even if it didn't fool him, might confuse him somewhat.

Listening intently, I thought I heard a shoe scrape across the floor. I tried to stop breathing so I could hear the slightest sound. I heard a shoe scrape again, and then I heard him breathing. Steady, slow, controlled and, he thought, undetectable.

At that moment, however, I wasn't wearing shoes, and I wasn't breathing, so the sounds I heard could only be coming from one of us.

And he was off to my left, coming closer.

He was working his way toward me, so I began to work my way backward. I moved slowly, but eventually made my way down to where the targets were. I got in among the target tracks, out of the chute, so that I could cross from chute to chute. Finally I was against the wall where the metal door was. Whoever my opponent was, he must have been inside one of the chutes by now. I worked my way down the wall to the main light switch.

When I hit the switch the room would be flooded with

light. At that point we'd both be momentarily blinded, but he'd know where I was. If he was where I thought he was—inside one of the target chutes—that made us even. If he was in another part of the room, that gave him the advantage, because I'd have to look for him. He would automatically fire at the light switch.

I took a deep breath and hit the switch. As the room was bathed in blinding light I hit the floor. His bullets chewed chunks out of the wall where my head had been. I squinted against the light, down the two center chutes. I could make out his figure, crouched in the same chute where I had previously squatted so painfully. I extended Wilhelmina straight out in front of me, in the accepted form, and fired down the chute.

There was no return fire.

I turned the intensity of the light down to a sub-normal level and walked over to the chute, to see who my would-be assassin was.

He was lying on his stomach in a pool of blood. His gun, what looked like a .38 Police Special, was lying further down the chute, thrown there when he was hit by my slugs.

When I turned him over I saw that he was the same guard who had let me into the building earlier that evening.

SIX

"We found the real guard in a closet, tied and gagged," Hawk told me.

It was later the same night and I had summoned him from a quiet night at home back to his office. He was livid until he found out the reason why.

"We've got a leak," he said after I told him the story. That struck him hard. AXE was his life, and anything that threatened it, threatened him.

"What was his story?"

"A man approached him to ask him something about the building. He started to answer, and the next thing he knew, everything went dark. He woke up in the closet with a headache."

"Can he identify the man who approached him?"

"Yes. We had him look at the body, and he made a positive identification."

"There had to be someone else, though. The man who approached him was not the man—or person—who hit him over the head."

"No," Hawk confirmed, "he was struck from behind, of that he was certain."

"I have to go to Switzerland," I reminded him, "so you're going to have to get someone else to work on this."

"No, I won't," he told me.

"Why?"

"I'll work on this myself," he answered.

It sounded more like a vow.

As I left his office I was thinking, I would hate to have David Hawk after me.

As I got off the plane in Switzerland I was wishing I was back in Washington, working with Hawk at finding the leak in AXE. I had my own assignment to work on, however, and I'd be much better off if I devoted all of my time and energy to it and nothing else.

When I reached the ski lodge where the competition was being held I asked if a Nikki Barnes had arrived yet.

The girl behind the desk was nice enough to look it up for me. "I'm sorry, there's no one by that name registered," she told me. Then she leaned her chin on her hands and asked, "Won't anyone else do?"

I flicked the tip of her nose with my finger and said, "If someone else would, it would be you. What's your name?"

"Around here they call me Angel."

"Okay, Angel, would you check the register one more time for me?"

"Sure."

It was just a thought. "Martin Leonard."

She bowed her head and scanned the book for me, then looked up with a happy smile on her face, glad that she could help.

"He's here. Arrived earlier today."

"Thanks, Angel. I'll see you later."

"I hope so."

I let a bellboy carry my bag to my room and tipped him. I decided to unpack, check out my room and then check out the bar. That was where I figured I'd find Martin Leonard.

Actually, I was interested in anyone who had been in

Atlantic City who was also here. I figured on buying Angel a drink later on, and getting her to supply me with a list of all of the arrivals of the last few days. I had brought a list with me of all of the competitors in Atlantic City, for comparison.

As a matter of course I checked my room for listening devices and found none.

I unpacked my bag, checked the kit in the false bottom, which would allow me to turn a television or a radio into a communications device. After that I showered, dressed, made sure Wilhelmina, Hugo and Pierre were all operable and accessible, and then went downstairs to find the bar.

Martin Leonard was well into a monumental drunk. He was telling anyone who would listen how he had almost won the Atlantic City tournament.

There were not that many people listening.

I thought it might be best to get him to his room before he made a complete fool of himself.

"Martin, if any officials happen to see you here, in this condition," I whispered to him urgently, "you could be disqualified from the competition before it even starts. Then you wouldn't be able to show them—"

"Right, show them," he said, cutting me off. "Okay, Nick, let's go to my room. Then you come back and you tell them about Atlantic City, okay?"

"Okay, Martin, okay."

I led him out of the bar to the front desk, where Angel was watching curiously.

"What room is Mr. Leonard in?" I asked her. After she told me I asked her what time she got off.

"In about an hour."

"Have a drink with me?"

"I'd love to."

"I'll see you then."

I steered Leonard to the elevator, and then to his room. It took us a while to locate his key, but between the two of us we finally found it. I got him into the room and stretched out on the bed. He was mumbling, but soon after he hit the mattress he was asleep. I loosened his tie and unbuttoned his shirt, but that was as far as I went to make him more comfortable.

The room was identical to mine, although he was two floors higher. I looked around idly, then decided that, since I was inside, I might as well take a better look around.

He hadn't yet unpacked his suitcase. It was sitting on a dresser, unlocked and open. I went through it without making a mess, which is the way a pro does a search. None of that dumping drawers on the floor and overturning pillows. That was for the movies and television.

I didn't really know what I was looking for, it was just an opportunity that was too good to pass up. I might have found something out of the ordinary for a chessplayer, something that might point him out as something more, but I found nothing.

Until I opened the night table drawer, right by the bed.

It was a Smith & Wesson .38, and it was right where he could reach it in case of an emergency.

What was a chess player doing with a gun?

I took it out and checked it, found it fully loaded. The simple fact that he had a gun was not in itself damaging. Lots of people have guns.

But it was a good thing for me to know.

SEVEN

"So you're a chess player?" Angel asked, surprised.

I nodded and answered, "What's surprising about that?"

It was a little over an hour since I'd left Leonard's room, and Angel and I were in the bar, getting acquainted.

She shrugged and said, "Oh, I don't know, you look more like an athlete than a chess player."

I had revised my original estimate of her age. She was lucky if she made twenty. Her face was remarkably fresh and young, with clear green eyes and a lovely, full-lipped, ready-to-smile mouth. She was slim, with small breasts, and very tall, at least five-ten.

"You look like a fashion model, so what are you doing behind the desk of a Swiss ski resort?" I asked her.

"Well, I just finished my last year at college, where I majored in fashion design, so you're not that far off, really," she told me.

"No desire to actually be a model?" I asked.

"Well, sure, I'd love it, but I'm too clumsy," she explained, shaking her head. "And I get nervous easily." She held up her hand, which was sweating, to demonstrate.

"Why are you nervous now?"

She shrugged. "I guess you make me nervous," she answered.

"There's no need for that," I assured her. I reached over to take her hand, but when I touched it she jumped.

"See?" she said, rubbing her hands together.

I reached over and very deliberately took her hand in mine.

"See," I said, mimicking her, "no damage. In fact, it feels kind of nice," I added, holding her right hand with mine, and rubbing it with my left.

She lowered her eyes shyly and picked up her crème de menthe with her other hand. I released her hand and picked up my bourbon. We clinked glasses and I said, "Here's to not being nervous."

"I'll drink to that," she agreed, and we both did.

"Tell me, how do you get along here?" I asked. "I mean, with the different language and all?"

"Oh, that's easy. I've been wanting to make this trip for some time, so I took the language as one of my minors. I can speak it almost perfectly."

She finished her drink and I held up my hand to the waiter for another.

"Just one more," she told me, "then I have to go back to the desk."

"All right," I agreed. When the waiter brought the fresh drinks I asked her, "And what time do you get off the desk for good?"

"At eight."

"Do you have any plans for dinner?" I inquired.

She shook her head. "I usually just have dinner sent to my room."

"Well then, would you have dinner with me tonight . . . in my room?"

"In your room?" she asked.

I leaned forward and whispered, "I promise I won't bite."

She sipped her drink while she thought it over, then

shyly agreed. I have always had a theory about shy girls being unexploded bombs. I was hoping to find out that evening if my theory was correct in this case.

"Have any of the other players registered since I arrived?" I asked.

She thought a moment and said, "No, not that I know of. There have been a couple of arrivals, but they didn't mention that they were part of the tournament."

"Was one of them a lady, dark-haired, about thirty, very pretty?"

"No, no one like that. Are you waiting for her to arrive? Is she your—"

"She's a friend," I told her, and that was all.

She seemed satisfied by the answer. "When does the contest start?" she asked.

"Tomorrow night. Tonight might be my last night to relax," I told her.

She smiled and said, "That sounds like a warning."

I smiled back and answered, "Well, it's not a threat, that's for sure."

EIGHT

After seeing Angel back to the desk, I went to my room for a heavy coat. I wanted to take a walk outside and see what the place was like. Just to be on the safe side, I put Wilhelmina in my coat pocket, where she'd be easy to get at if I needed her.

I went out the front door and began to circle around to the back. I went through the parking lot, which was only half full of cars. It looked virtually the same way it had looked when I had arrived in my rented vehicle.

Around back was where most of the ski equipment was kept. The pro shop was empty except for the clerk who worked there. It was about five P.M. and many of the guests were probably taking in an early dinner.

I walked as far as the ski lift, which was still operating. As far as I could see there was no one on the way up or down. I was pretty sure I knew where everything was now, so I started back to the hotel.

The snow beneath my feet was hard packed, and when the bullet hit it and went through, it made an audible, scrunching sound. I threw myself into motion, pulling Wilhelmina from my pocket at the same time. I rolled about ten yards, then came up on my knees with my gun held out in front of me, hoping for a target.

I've been shot at so many times by unknown persons

from unknown directions that the drill had become the same. They take one, maybe two shots, and by the time you recover from evasive action, you've got nothing to shoot at.

In this case, there was just the one shot but true to form, there was no target for me to shoot at once I'd gotten myself set.

Remaining on guard until I was fairly sure the immediate danger had passed, I then retraced my steps back to where I had been when the bullet hit.

I searched the ground for a few moments, looking for the entry hole. When I found it I put Wilhelmina back in my coat pocket and brought out Hugo. Using my faithful knife I dug for the bullet. I had to dig down about eight inches in a diagonal direction before I finally found it. It had entered the snow cleanly and had suffered virtually no disfigurement.

It was a .38 caliber slug, the same caliber as the gun in Martin Leonard's hotel room.

I dropped the bullet into my coat pocket and put Hugo away. I stood up and looked around, finding no one in site. My assailant was gone and there were apparently no witnesses. Nobody knew about the incident except for him and me.

I walked back to the hotel and looked into the pro shop. The clerk was still the only one inside. I opened the door and went in.

"Good evening," I greeted.

He stared blankly at me, obviously not comprehending what I was saying—or not wanting to.

He was a tall lad in his mid-twenties, dark-haired with a lot of it curling on his collar. He had a dark, bushy mustache and, beneath his shirt, I sensed a bunch of bulging muscles. His eyes were brown and, at least for the moment, blank.

"Do you understand English?" I asked, but still got no response.

I pointed to the telephone and he nodded. I needed an interpreter and I knew where to find one. I dialed the desk and Angel answered.

"Hi, Angel?"

"Nick?" she asked. I'd signed in and introduced myself to her as Nicholas Crane, the name I'd used in Atlantic City.

"It's me. I'm in the pro shop and I'm having a hard time communicating with the fella down here—"

"Michael?"

"Yeah, I guess." I turned to him and said, "Michael?" He nodded, and I told her that's who it was. "I want to ask him a couple of questions. Could you interpret for me?"

"Well, I can't leave the desk, but if you put him on I'll do my best."

"Great. Ask him if he's seen anyone else beside me around the area in the last, oh, twenty minutes or so."

"Why?"

"Just do it. *Please?*"

I handed Michael the phone, and when he found out who it was his face lit up into a great big smile. He listened a moment, then answered her while shaking his head. I got the general idea.

He handed the phone back to me and Angel told me, "He says he hasn't seen anyone in the past half hour, not even you."

That much was true. The first time I'd looked into the shop he hadn't looked up, so he hadn't seen me, either. If that were the case, there was no need to ask him anything further.

"All right, that's it then," I told her.

"That's all?" she asked.

"Yes. See you for dinner."

"Nick—" she began, but I cut her off by hanging up. I turned to Michael and waved a hand in thanks. He stared back at me, and I noticed a subtle change in his appearance.

His eyes were no longer blank, and the expression they held was one of intense dislike.

NINE

About an hour before I was to meet Angel for dinner, I stopped by Martin Leonard's room to see how he was feeling.

He answered the door clad in a terrycloth bathrobe, rubbing at his soaking hair with a towel. Fresh from the shower, obviously, trying to shake the cobwebs clear.

"Mr. Crane," he said, from beneath the towel.

"Martin. How are you feeling?"

He stopped rubbing his head and frowned at me a moment, then understood. "Are you the one who brought me up here?" he asked.

"That's right."

He stepped back and said, "Come on in and close the door, will you?"

I shut the door behind me as he was going into the bathroom.

"Let me get dried off. I'll be with you in a minute," he told me.

"Take your time."

As soon as he closed the door behind him I opened the top drawer of the night table.

The gun wasn't there.

In my business you learn not to jump to conclusions. I would rather have the gun in my hands, to check and see if it were fired, then find him guilty simply because the gun wasn't where I last saw it.

I closed the drawer quietly and sat on the bed. He came out of the bathroom wearing a pair of pants and nothing else. His torso was so skinny I could see his ribs and breastbone. He went to a dresser and took out a T-shirt.

"I guess I should thank you," he said, putting the shirt on. "Was I making a fool of myself?"

"Not exactly," I lied.

"Like as not, I was."

He sat on the bed to put on a pair of socks, then put a hand to his head and went, *"Whew,* I must have really tied one on."

"You've recovered much quicker than I would have thought," I told him.

He got his socks on and said, "I've had lots of practice. Hey, what's say we have dinner together, huh?"

"Sorry," I told him, getting up, "I've already made plans for the evening."

"Scored already, huh? Yeah, I recognized you for a quick worker in Atlantic City. You latched onto that Barnes broad pretty quickly. Got another one now, huh? What are you gonna do when the Barnes broad shows up here?"

It was apparently a problem he'd never had, and he was interested.

"That's my business," I told him.

He turned and looked at me, then held up his hands and said, "Okay, okay, don't get touchy. I was just asking? Drawing's tomorrow night, right?"

"Right."

"Okay. If I don't see you before then, then I'd like to say good luck," he said as I started to leave, then added to himself, "Jesus, I need a drink."

That was the last thing he needed, but I kept my

mouth shut and left, regretting that I hadn't had a chance to do a quick search of the entire room for that gun.

When I got back to my room I had about a half an hour before Angel would arrive for dinner. I called room service and ordered dinner for two to be sent up—at nine o'clock. By seven-fifty I was shaved, showered, powdered and primped.

She arrived promptly at eight.

"Being nervous didn't stop you from being on time," I observed, opening the door to her knock.

"Not only am I on time," she pointed out, walking past me, "but I don't think I'm nervous anymore."

I shut the door and said, "That's good."

She was wearing a green dress, which went well with her red hair and brought out her eyes more. I was struck again at how tall and thin she was, but noticed that she had excellent legs.

"You look and smell delicious," I told her.

"Thank you."

She sat on the couch and I noticed that her skirt length was just below the knee. I wondered if her knees were bony.

She looked around, as if she noticed something missing.

"I thought we were having dinner?" she asked.

"We are. I asked them to bring it up at nine o'clock."

"Nine?"

I nodded, then offered, "I could call them back and tell them to rush it . . . if you're hungry, that is."

She thought a moment, then said, "No, I guess nine o'clock gives us enough time."

I sat next to her and commented, "I guess you really aren't shy, anymore, huh?"

She moved closer so our thighs were touching and answered, "I should have qualified it when I said I was shy.

I'm shy—initially." She put her arms around my neck and added, "I get over it very quickly." Then she kissed me.

Her tongue came alive in my mouth and I reacted to it. I reached behind her and opened her dress. There was no bra to fumble with as I ran my hands over her bare back. The flesh was smooth and cool, but she was heating up quickly. Without breaking the kiss we managed to peel her dress off, and then her panties. She hadn't worn any stockings, and simply kicked her shoes away.

She broke the kiss and said, "The bedroom."

I pushed her back on the couch and began to unbutton my shirt.

"Right here," I told her.

She watched me undress boldly, with her hands folded behind her head. It thrust her small breasts forward, their rust colored tips growing hard. There was no trace of nervousness now, and I wondered if that had all been an act. When my clothes were completely gone, she certainly didn't seem at a loss for what to do next. I allowed her to work over me for a while, then pushed her back down on the couch and began to explore her with my mouth. Her mouth was eager and hot and not easy to abandon, even momentarily, but I had to move on. I kissed her neck, then went to her breasts and teased her nipples before sucking them hard. As I worked my way lower she began to writhe beneath me. After a few moments she began to moan, "Oh, Nick, I want you in me now, right now."

I raised myself above her and she spread her long, lovely legs to allow me easy access. It couldn't have been easier as I plunged myself into her warm, wet cavity. Once I had achieved penetration, she closed those legs around me and began to rake my back with her nails. We achieved climax together, during which I bit her lightly on the shoulder.

After a few moments, when we both had our breathing under control and I was kissing the freckles between her breasts, she said, "You lied."

"About what?" I asked startled.

"Remember when you first invited me to your room for dinner?"

"Yes."

"You promised," she giggled, pulling my face close to hers, "that you wouldn't bite me," and then proceeded to take her revenge on various portions of my anatomy.

TEN

Angel stayed until about six in the morning, when she had to go to work. She asked if we could have breakfast together, but I nixed it by saying I was going to sleep late, then meet some of the other competitors. After she left I thought about how pleasant the night had been, and I was sorry I had told her that I was going to sleep late. I wanted to keep her happy because, along with being a lovely girl, she was also a contact in the hotel, as well as an interpreter.

About an hour later I dressed in a blue turtleneck, jeans and black loafers. I threw a jacket over the sweater, mainly to cover Wilhelmina. After yesterday's incident, I didn't want any distance between her and me.

I was in the lobby by nine, and Angel was behind the desk, so I told her that I couldn't sleep for thinking about her.

"What a sweet lie."

"You want to discuss lies?" I asked her. "How about your shy act?"

She lowered her eyes and said, "Yes, well, I'm sorry about that, but it worked, didn't it?"

"In what way?"

"I got you into bed, didn't I?"

"You got me—" I began, about to explain that it was the other way around.

"Okay, we went to bed together," she relented. "That was my goal, anyway, right from the first moment I saw you. Are you sorry I'm not the sweet, shy thing you thought I was?"

"Who said I ever thought that?"

"C'mon, I had you fooled. Admit it."

"Never. Any more competitors arrive?" I asked.

"You mean your girl friend?" she asked, shaking her head. "I checked as soon as I came on." She leaned on the desk and said, "Nick, if you've got something going for yourself, don't worry, I won't blow it for you. If it doesn't work out, I'll be around. Okay?"

I didn't know if I was ready for this major turnaround in personality. I'd never admit it to her, but I had thought she was a shrinking violet, right up until the time we kissed. After that it became plain she wasn't what she had pretended to be, but what about now. Was this liberated, understanding young woman before me also a put on?

"I'll keep you in mind," I promised.

Someone came up to the desk and she went to work. I went into the restaurant to see if there was anyone there that I might know from Atlantic City. The only familiar face was that of Martin Leonard, who had what looked like a Bloody Mary in front of him. He waved me over.

He wasn't alone; there was a man and a woman with him, and he rose to make introductions.

"Nick, this is Mr. and Mrs. Andre Dupree, from France. They are both here to compete. This is my fellow American, Nick Crane."

"Ah, a husband and wife team," I remarked. I shook hands with Andre, who was a dapper little man in his early forties with a short clipped mustache and graying sideburns.

"Happy to meet you," he said with a heavy French accent.

His wife extended her hand to me, and her eyes looked me over with open frankness.

"Martine," she told me as I took her hand, making it clear that she was not "just" Mrs. Dupree.

She was somewhat younger than her husband. She had rather large, expressive brown eyes and a pouty, sexy mouth. Her eyes were heavily made-up, but to perfection, so that it enhanced their power. Though she was seated, I judged that she was also taller than her husband. The way she was looking me up and down, I sensed a time bomb looking for somewhere to explode. Under normal circumstances, I would have loved to have been alone with her when she did, but I didn't need husband and wife trouble right now.

"Martine," I repeated, "it's a pleasure."

"Sit, Nick. Have a drink," Martin invited. From the look of his eyes, the one he was working on was not his first. My file on him said he didn't drink until after a match, but he seemed to have abandoned any such rule. True, there were to be no matches today, but the drawing was coming up, and that signalled the beginning of the competition. By that time, he would be thoroughly wasted, I was sure.

I sat, and I had a Bloody Mary, because I wanted to get to know as many of the competitors as I could. I'd meet some through Martin, some through the Duprees, and some on my own.

"Your name is not familiar to me, Mr. Crane," Andre Dupree told me.

"Please, call me Nick."

"As you wish."

"I told you, pal," Martin said, referring to the time in Atlantic City when he'd said practically the same thing.

I accepted my Bloody Mary from the waiter, than shrugged at Dupree's remark and said, "I tend to keep a low profile."

"I beg your pardon?" Dupree said politely.

"He stays out of the spotlight," Martin offered, and the Frenchman seemed to understand that.

"Well, Martine," I began, trying to steer the subject away from me. "How did you become interested in chess? Through Andre?"

"Oh, no," she replied, "even as a child I played chess. I love it. I find it such a, a sexy game, don't you?" She asked me that question, making it plain it was not for anyone but me.

"Martine," her husband scolded.

"Darling, Mr. Crane is a man of the world. He is not easily shocked," she told him. "Especially not by anything that a woman might say or do. Are you, Nick?"

I could almost hear her ticking, now. It was plain that their marriage was not exactly perfect.

"I've found it to be my experience that a woman may say or do anything," I replied, "and that it would not be wise to be surprised."

She clapped her hands together in delight and gushed, "Oh, how delightfully put!"

Her husband frowned, but I wasn't sure if it was meant for me or for her. I was looking for a way to get out, and I found it. At the front desk I saw Nikki signing in.

"Excuse me, please. I see someone I want to talk to."

"It was a pleasure meeting you," Martine said quickly, extending her hand. I took it, looked at her husband and replied, "It was very nice meeting you both!"

As I approached the front desk, Angel saw me coming and put a smirk on her face. I made a face at her and she smiled. At least I wasn't going to have to worry about her reading more into a night in bed than she should. Besides, I was willing to wager that muscle-bound Michael would be around for whenever she needed him.

"This is cutting it kind of fine, isn't it?" I remarked to Nikki.

She turned her head to see who was speaking, and

when she saw me she smiled brilliantly. Her eyes looked gray today, and I was once again struck by how much impact they could have on a man.

"Nick!" she said happily, reaching up to kiss me lightly. "How nice."

"How are you, Nikki?"

"I'm fine. I had a little trouble getting away from home, but I finally made it."

"Nothing serious, I hope."

She wrinkled her lovely nose and assured me that it was just a little business. I wondered idly what her business was. We had never gotten around to discussing that.

"When did you arrive?" she asked.

"Yesterday. Let me take your bags," I offered.

"I can have someone do that," Angel said, helpfully. I looked at her and knew she was teasing.

"That's okay," I assured her. "I can handle it."

Nikki looked at Angel and said, "Thank you, dear," when Angel gave her the key to her room. I noticed that she was on the same floor I was, courtesy of Angel, no doubt. I smiled at her behind Nikki's back and she in turn stuck her tongue out at me and wiggled it.

In the elevator with Nikki I realized that she was as tall as Angel, but that the two women were built totally different. Nikki was full-bodied, with lush breasts and buttocks, while Angel was almost flat-chested and had an ass that could only be described as boyish. Yet both women were exciting to look at and be with.

"What floor are you on?" Nikki asked.

"The same as you, love."

She leaned her head on my shoulder and said, "Did you slip that young girl something for that?"

I almost laughed, but controlled myself and said, "Something like that."

"Is that your plan, then?"

"What?"

"To distract me from my game?"

"My plan is to keep you distracted when you're not concentrating on your game," I told her. "You don't think I'd use sex to try and win a competition, do you?"

"My goodness, of course not," she replied sarcastically.

Her room was on the same floor, all right, but at opposite ends. Angel at work again. She had a marvelous sense of humor, that girl.

Once we were in her room she turned and bumped into me, as she had done the first time we met. I dropped her bags and took her into my arms. She smelled of perfume and perspiration, and as we began to get more and more amorous she pushed me away and said, "Not now, Nick. Let me get cleaned up and settled, and we'll have lunch. Do you ski?"

"Yes."

"Good. We'll hit the slopes together and have some fun. Tonight we can come back here and have a nice, quiet dinner."

"In between all of that, if it doesn't interfere with your plans any, we might as well stop in at the drawing, seeing as how that's the real reason we're here," I reminded her.

She laughed behind her hand and said, "I completely forgot about it. See, you've distracted me already," she accused.

"Well then, I'll get out of here so I don't distract you any further."

ELEVEN

I went back down to the desk and Angel smirked at me again. "I need a favor," I told her.

"I put you on the same floor together," she told me. "Now what do you want, a double room?"

"No, wise-ass, I need a real favor."

"Okay, ask."

"When people check in, do they all tell you if they're here for the competition?"

"They all have, so far."

"Would you make me a complete list of everyone who has arrived, then add the arrivals for the rest of the day?"

"You want a complete list of all the competitors?"

"Right."

"Couldn't you get that from the organizers?"

"I'd much rather get it from you," I told her, leaning over the desk.

"It's going to cost you," she warned.

"I'm willing to pay you any price," I promised.

She said, *"Hmm,"* and then, "Okay, you've got it."

"Listen, has Belnikov arrived yet? He's the Soviet Master. When he arrives it'll be with an entourage, probably a couple of big, burly types on each side of him."

She made a face. "Nothing like that has arrived yet, Nick."

"When he does, could you find me and let me know. I'm anxious to meet him."

"Okay, will do."

"Thanks." I touched her hand and left the vicinity of the desk.

I had the better part of an hour to kill, and it was too early for a drink—for me, that is—so I decided to kill it over a couple of cups of coffee.

The Duprees were gone, but Martin Leonard was still there in the same booth, and he had graduated from Bloody Marys. He waved me over to join him.

"Just coffee," I told the waiter.

"What did you think of that Martine Dupree, eh?" he asked with his tongue hanging to the table.

"A very nice package, but trouble."

"Dynamite's the word, partner, pure dynamite. Her husband's got no control of her, and she usually tears right through most of the competition."

"On the board?"

"And on the mattress," he added, winking. He had a remarkable capacity for booze. He should have been rigid already, but he'd probably last until late afternoon. I hoped it wasn't going to turn out to be my job to lug him to his room everyday.

He waved an arm at the waiter and caught my glance. "You don't approve."

"I wouldn't normally have an opinion, but since you mentioned it, no, I don't."

"Well, I don't really give a damn," he told me, without rancor.

"I know you don't, Martin, that's why I wouldn't have offered my opinion."

The waiter brought his drink and, with a full glass in his hand, he suggested, "Hey, c'mon, Nick, let's stay friends, huh? Listen, I notice you do pretty well with the ladies. I don't even think Martine will tax your abilities."

I was about to answer when he looked past me and apparently liked what he saw. I turned to see Nikki bearing down on us.

"Miss Barnes," he greeted when she reached the table. We both rose and she slid in on my side.

"Hello, Mr. Leonard. How are you?"

"I'm fine, just dandy," he said, and took a healthy swig of his drink to prove it.

"That was quick," I told her.

"I was impatient," she answered. "I abandoned the age old woman's weapon of keeping the man waiting."

"Hooray for women's lib," I cheered.

We both looked at Martin Leonard then and found him grinning happily at our exchange, as if he were a kid who had just been let in on a grown-up secret.

"Would you like a drink?" he asked her.

She made a face and said, "Too early."

"Not for me," he assured her, then took another healthy swig to prove that, too.

"How about some coffee?" I suggested. "It's going to be cold on the slopes."

"I'll take some hot chocolate."

When her hot chocolate came we started talking chess with Martin who, surprisingly enough, was still able to hold up his end of the conversation.

"Belnikov's the man to beat, naturally," Nikki commented.

"He can be beat," Martin said confidently.

"Have you ever played him?" she asked.

"Sure."

"Have you ever beat him?"

"He got lucky," Martin lamented. I looked at her, trying to warn her not to pursue it.

She was sharp, though. She'd already sized Martin Leonard up. He was the kind of man who would always find some excuse with which to explain away a defeat.

"Just take my word for it," he told us. *"The man can be beat."*

I finished my coffee and Nikki her hot chocolate. Martin was starting to slip into a haze, so we decided to make for the slopes. I didn't want to ask Nikki to help me get him to his room.

"We'll see you later, Martin."

"Have a ball, you two. Don't break a leg," he told us, then laughed uproariously at what he thought was a great joke.

We entered the pro shop from within the hotel, and checked out not only the ski equipment, but appropriate jackets. I hoisted both pairs of skis onto my shoulder and we made our way to the ski lift.

On the ride up Nikki commented, "I wonder how long he'll last, drinking like that?"

"I'm more interested in seeing what kind of shape he'll be in tomorrow, for his first match."

She shook her head wonderingly. "I've been in a few tournaments with him before Atlantic City. He always seems to be ready for his matches. Then again, I've never seen him drink quite like this before."

"You haven't played Belnikov before?" I asked.

She shook her head. "I'm looking forward to it, win or lose. In fact, I'm just looking forward to watching him play."

"Do you know any of the other competitors?"

"Some of them. I'm not sure yet of who is going to be here."

"How about the Duprees, Andre and Martine?"

"Martine Dupree," she repeated, "is a maneater. She's got that poor husband of hers wrapped right around her little finger. He's so in love with her he'll forgive her anything, just so long as she stays with him. Watch out for her, Nick. She'll be after you like a bee after honey."

"We met this morning."

"Then she's already zeroed in on you," she assured me.

"She was looking me up and down like something on display," I admitted.

"And you were looking back, weren't you?"

"I have to admit, the lady presents a pretty impressive package," I said, truthfully.

She squeezed my arm and said ferociously, "Well, I'll see if I can't give you all you can handle. In fact, maybe I'll just have a little talk with Martine."

"A fight to the finish with me as the prize?"

"Are you worth that?" she asked. "No, maybe just a little chat, to arrange our priorities."

We reached the top and all such conversation was suspended. Neither one of us professed to being premier skiers, so we forwent the "big hill" and took a nice leisurely run down the smaller one. She was very graceful on skis, and I had no doubt that if she put her mind to it she could become an excellent skier.

Once we reached the bottom we removed our goggles and paused to catch our breath.

"Whoo, that was fun," she exclaimed.

"You want to go for another run?" I asked her.

She hugged her arms and said, "Do you?"

"Not really."

"Good. I'm cold. I think I'm ready for another hot chocolate, followed by something a little stronger."

"You're on."

We went back to the pro shop and returned all of the equipment to the silent Michael. He gave me that familiar blank stare, but something flickered in his eyes when he looked at Nikki. She gave him a warm smile and said thank you, then forgot him and took my arm. Once again I got the feeling that I was never going to be one of Michael's favorite people.

In the bar Martin Leonard was not in evidence. There

were several people present that Nikki seemed to know, however, and we ended up at a table with a few of the other competitors.

At one point I caught Angel's eye from the desk and she signalled that she hadn't seen Belnikov yet.

I wondered what was keeping him, and what I would do if he just never showed up.

TWELVE

Nikki wore a high-necked pantsuit to the drawing that evening and was absolutely stunning. Martine Dupree wore a gown, slit up the side and cut low in front, exhibiting a lot of skin. It was impressive, but she was upstaged by Nikki's dignity, grace and beauty. Martine had flash, but the rest was all Nikki's.

The drawing was before dinner, and it began with a cocktail party. Martin Leonard was present with a glass in his hand, looking a little worse for wear, but he was lucid, which was a surprise. Andrew Dupree was following his wife around the room, and every so often she'd send him to the bar for another drink. It was during one of these trips to the bar that she approached Nikki and me.

"Nikki, darling, are you hogging this beautiful man all for yourself?" she asked. She was built somewhere in between Nikki and Angel. Her breasts were small, but perfectly rounded, like two melons. She wasn't as tall as Nikki, but she was wearing high, spiked heels to make up the difference. The two women embraced the way women who don't like each other usually do.

"All for myself," Nikki answered her. "And I intend to keep it that way, darling. Oh, here comes your husband."

Martine made a face, but put on a smile for him when he handed her the fresh drink.

"I wonder what can be keeping the great Belnikov," Andre Dupree said.

"I hope he shows," Nikki said. "The whole competition would be a waste if he didn't. Do you think something might have happened to him?" she asked.

"I hope not," I told her, and she didn't know the half of it. "Can I get you a fresh drink?" I asked her.

"Thank you."

I took her glass and made for the bar. I had intentions of checking with Angel, but as I approached the bar I saw her at the entrance to the room looking around. I got the drinks and then walked over to her. When she saw me approaching she looked relieved.

"Nick, I've been looking for you. That man's arrived."

"Belnikov?"

She nodded. "Bodyguards and all. In fact, they didn't even let him come to the desk. He stayed in the car while some woman with a hatchet face came in and registered. When they had the room number they brought him in and went straight to the elevator. Nick, the men with him had their hands inside their jackets and they kept looking around. It reminded me of a gangster movie, you know, where the Feds are trying to protect the witness?"

I nodded, indicating that I had seen some of the movies she was talking about.

She leaned closer to me and asked, "Are you a Fed, Nick?"

It was unexpected, but I reacted rather well to it.

"What makes you ask that?" I asked, hoping I sounded more amused than I felt.

"Well, you were so interested in knowing as soon as he got here, and you knew he'd have those bodyguards—"

"He's a very important man in Russia, Angel. Of course they'd protect him. Besides, I'm just very interested in meeting the man, that's all. Do you remember what room he's in?"

She smiled and said, "I was waiting for you to ask. He's in 1511, on the top floor. It's the largest room we have."

"Thanks, love."

When I got back to where I had left Nikki, the Duprees had gone elsewhere and she was cornered by three gentlemen.

"Excuse me, please?" I said, elbowing my way past them.

"I thought you got lost," she told me, accepting the drink.

"And these gentlemen were going to help you find me?" I asked, looking all three of them in the eye. They all suddenly remembered someplace else they had to be, and we were left alone.

"What took you so long?"

"I wanted to check on Belnikov. He's only just arrived."

"Well, that's a relief. Even if he doesn't come down for the drawing, at least he's here."

"Speaking of the drawing, it looks like they're about to start," I told her.

There were quite a few competitors, so it was some time before all of the names were finally matched. Nikki had drawn someone we didn't know. She said she had some accounts of past competitions that she had brought with her, so she'd be able to look him up once we went to her room.

Martin Leonard had drawn a name I was unfamiliar with, but that Nikki knew.

"He shouldn't have any problem getting past him," she told me, shaking her head. "That is, depending on what kind of shape he's in."

I listened while the rest of the names were called out, and recognized a few from Atlantic City. The files Hawk had prepared on the Atlantic City competitors were in my room. I'd have to separate them later, now that I knew who was here.

Andre Dupree had drawn one of the female competitors for his first match. In fact, aside from Nikki and Martine, I'd only seen one other, old woman present, but she didn't appear to be the one drawn by Andre, so there were at least four.

Martine had drawn an opponent who's name I was very familiar with.

She drew me.

THIRTEEN

The cocktail party went on for an hour or so after the drawing, and then started to thin out.

"Nick, I'm going to go on up to my room and order dinner," Nikki told me.

"I'll come with you."

"No, you wait down here for a while. I want to get myself ready. Come up in about a half an hour. Mingle, meet some more people," she told me, then seemed to have a second thought and added, "but stay away from Martine."

"I'll watch my step," I assured her. She kissed me shortly and left.

Belnikov never showed, so I could only assume that he would pick up the name of his opponent in the morning. The first match would begin at ten. I wouldn't have to sit across a chessboard from the lovely Martine until two.

I tried my best, but eventually Martine was able to corner me. Andre was nowhere in sight, so I assumed he had been sent to his room.

"Well, well, my erstwhile opponent," she announced, bearing down on me.

She seemed just the least bit drunk, unless it was just an excuse to lean on me heavily, which she did. She smelled of gin and perfume, and the contact was not all that unpleasant. Her breasts were very firm against my chest.

"I want to warn you, Nick, that I play to win," she said, her face very close to mine. The room was emptying out but there were still some people present, yet she didn't seem inhibited.

"Are we talking about chess?" I asked her.

"*Hmm,* you're a clever man. I could make you feel very good, you know," she told me, slipping a hand inside my jacket.

"In exchange for what?" I asked. I had a funny feeling I knew where she was headed.

"I could make you forget everything else," she went on.

"Including the match tomorrow?" I asked.

"I told you, I like to win. I use every means at my command."

"Including sex."

"It's one of my most potent weapons," she assured me.

"Is that the one that keeps poor Andre on the hook?" I asked.

She made a face. "He loves me. I don't want to talk about him, I want to talk about us."

"The only time we become *us,* Martine," I told her, "is when we sit down across that board from each other tomorrow."

Apparently she wasn't used to being rejected, because she appeared surprised. "You are joking?" she asked.

"No," I told her, removing her hand from inside my jacket, "I am not. Excuse me, please."

Once I walked past her I didn't bother to turn around and look back, but I was willing to bet that, had I done so, I would have seen her standing there, shaking her head in disbelief.

Under any other circumstances I would have been

only too happy to take her up on her offer, but I didn't like her and she'd made it very easy to turn her down. Could she want to win a chess match that badly?

I wondered how many she had already won with that offer?

Enough to get her here, that was obvious.

FOURTEEN

By the time I got out of the elevator, I'd forgotten Martine Dupree. I had visions of sugar plums and Nikki Barnes dancing in my head. I had several different images of what she would be dressed in. When I reached the door I found it ajar. Unlocked doors are a familiar hazard in my business, but that extra sense of mine told me that in this case it was intentional. In spite of that, I still walked in carefully; when the roof didn't fall in on my head, I decided I was safe.

Nikki was lying on the floor on her stomach, with one leg up in the air behind her, swinging back and forth at the knee. She was concentrating on some papers spread out in front of her; nearby there was a chessboard set up. Apparently, she didn't have in mind what I had in mind, because instead of a negligee, which I had expected, she was wearing a sweatshirt and jeans.

"You made it," she said without looking behind.

"I almost didn't," I told her.

She turned her head and asked, "What's that mean?"

"Martine."

"Stop standing there with your mouth open and come lie down beside me. We've got work to do. I'm trying to find out something about my opponent's game, and I can help you with Martine's. Oh, I've ordered dinner

63

and it should be up here soon. What happened with Martine?"

"She offered me her body in exchange for the match tomorrow," I told her. The papers she had on the floor were typewritten and newspaper accounts of past competitions. If she were a horse player, you could say she was handicapping.

"And you said no? That must have crushed her. She hasn't been unsuccessful with that ploy very often."

"She's used it before?"

She nodded with her chin resting in her palm, leafing through papers. "Not too often. She must be worried about you."

"She's never seen me play," I argued.

"You have an aura about you, Nick. It says 'I know what I'm doing at all times.' She must have read your aura and decided you were dangerous. She'll do almost anything to win," she warned.

"How's her game?"

"I can show you," she told me, abandoning the papers in front of her and moving to the chessboard. We settled down on opposite sides of the board and she proceeded to play me the way she said Martine would. From time to time she'd suggest I make a move other than the one I did.

"You play the perfect type of game to beat her, Nick," she told me. "She can't take constant pressure. She's not a counterpuncher. If you get her backing up early, you'll have her."

"Right now, I'd rather have you," I told her. I got up from the board and pushed her down on her back on the floor. I pushed her sweatshirt up around her neck, revealing her large breasts. I began kissing those marvelously firm mounds of flesh and had just started working on her nipples when there was a knock at the door. I ignored it the first time, but it was followed by a second knock.

"Who is it?" Nikki called out while I continued to work on her breasts.

"Room service," a voice called out.

"Nick, the dinner's here," she told me.

I nodded, but kept at her.

"Nick," she said, grabbing my head and turning my face so she could see me, "I'm hungry!"

I made a face at her and allowed her to get to her feet. She opened the door and allowed the bellboy to wheel the dinner cart in. He started to fuss with chairs, but Nikki told him not to bother.

He stood waiting and I was tempted to see if we could outlast him, but I finally gave in. I got up, dug into my pocket and tipped him. Nikki signed the check and he left.

"I have to admit," I told her, "that I'm hungry, too. What did you order?"

"See?" she told me. "Stomach first, other parts of the anatomy later."

She'd ordered simple: steak, boiled potatoes, vegetables, a pot of coffee and a bottle of wine. I brought two chairs over to the cart and we started eating.

"What did you find out about your opponent?" I asked her.

"Mediocre," she answered. "He's Dutch, very young and inexperienced."

"He got this far, didn't he?"

"He'll get no further," she said, confidently.

"It isn't wise to underestimate your opponent," I told her.

"I'm not underestimating him," she insisted. "I've got him pegged exactly right. Unless he springs some great surprise on me, I shouldn't have any problem getting past him."

"I can't fault your attitude."

"Thank you," she smiled.

After dinner we got back on the floor . . . to play

chess. We went through some variations and I was lucky that I was able to stay with her. I had Evan Clarke to thank for that. He'd taught me well.

Once we were done experimenting she proposed that we play a game for real, and we settled on a stake of ten bucks.

After more than an hour had passed she said, "Nick, how about declaring a draw?"

I was studying the board intently. "Just a little while longer, love. I think I can get you," I told her.

"You don't have to get me," she told me, "you can have me."

When I looked up, she had removed her sweatshirt and positioned herself so that I could see her breasts above the board.

I carried her to the bedroom, where I set her down on the bed and removed her jeans. I shed my own clothes and joined her on the bed. She pushed me onto my back and began to explore my body with her hands, mouth and tongue. The pressure of her body moved around. One moment her breasts were pressed against my chest, the next moment they were lying heavily on my thighs. She teased my manhood with her nipples and tongue until I couldn't lie still any longer. I pulled her up beside me and began to explore her body the way she had done mine. I worked her from head to toe, but my favorite spot was her breasts.

Finally, I decided to put foreplay aside and get right to the heart of the matter. I raised myself above her and was about to enter her when she stopped me.

"What's wrong?" I asked.

"I-I'm not sure I should let you," she told me, her face serious.

"Why not?"

"Well, we could end up playing each other for the championship, Nick," she told me, and then she couldn't hide her smile any longer and I knew she was teasing me. "I might as well save something to bargain with."

I proceeded to leave her with nothing she could offer me that I hadn't already had.

FIFTEEN

Belnikov's first match wasn't until three in the afternoon, just after mine. I wanted to try and see him before then, but found out from Angel that it wasn't going to be all that easy.

"You got time for a cup of coffee?" I asked her the next morning at the desk.

"Sure." She turned to the man behind her and said something I didn't understand, then came with me.

"Has Belnikov been down?" I asked her.

"Haven't seen any sign of him since he got here, and nobody can get in to see him."

"Who's tried?" I was intrigued.

"Several of the competitors have called on his room and have been turned away. Some of them tried to get in to see him through us. You know, I'd call up and announce them? The woman on the phone—the one with a hatchet face—said that 'Comrade Belnikov is seeing no one'."

This was going to present a problem. I had to identify myself to Belnikov by giving him the prearranged sign, a spoken chess move. Not any move, but the next to last move he made in the match that won him the championship. How was I going to do that if I couldn't get close to him? I certainly couldn't depend on getting far enough in the tournament so that I'd end up playing him.

I couldn't do it on the phone, either; he was going to have to be able to recognize me.

"You look like you have such problems," Angel said, interrupting my reverie.

The waiter came with the coffees and she asked him to bring her a piece of dry, whole wheat toast.

"Is that how you keep your figure?" I asked.

She smiled, then said, "Speaking of figures, you've got a couple of stunners in the competition—your friend, Miss Barnes, and the Frenchwoman. She knocked Michael off last night, you know."

"How do you know she slept with him?" I asked.

"He told me."

"He told you he slept with one of the guests. Couldn't that get him fired?"

"Oh, Michael trusts me. We're friends," she said.

I couldn't read anything into the way she said that, so I didn't bother worrying about it. "Angel, you're going to have to help me," I said in a more serious tone.

"Oh. Another favor? Your debts are piling up."

"I know, I know. Don't worry, you'll get paid. Look, has Belnikov ordered breakfast sent up to his room yet?"

"No, but what makes you think he will?"

"With the security around him as tight as it's been so far? It makes sense, doesn't it?"

"I guess."

"When he calls, I want to bring it up."

"Nick, why are you so—"

"I know I'm asking a lot of you, Angel, and I'm going to ask more. Don't ask me any questions, please. Just help me."

She looked at me for a few moments, sipping her coffee slowly.

"You'll need a white coat. I can get one from

Michael. I'll have him bring the tray and the jacket up to the fifteenth floor in the service elevator. You can meet him there."

"Is it visible from the door of Belnikov's room?" I asked.

"No, it's not. Do you need anything else?"

"I didn't want to make her any more curious than she already was, but I was going to need some kind of a disguise. Something that would allow me to go unrecognized by the people with Belnikov when they saw me later, yet something I could remove so Belnikov could see what I really looked like.

I decided to do what I could without her, and told her, "No, nothing else. I'll go to my room and wait for you to call. Thanks, love."

"Don't mention it to anyone. But at the very least I'm going to expect an explanation—eventually."

I cupped her chin in my hand as I rose and repeated, "Eventually." Then I went back to my room to wait for her call and to see what I could do about a disguise.

SIXTEEN

By the time Angel's call came, I had disguised myself somewhat by changing my hair style, stuffing my cheeks with cotton and creating a mustache from small locks of my own hair and ordinary house glue.

I hung up and changed my clothes, putting on a pair of pants that were the same color as the hotel staff's and a pale shirt that wouldn't stand out beneath the white waiter's jacket. Before leaving the room, I checked out my disguise in the mirror, then headed for the fifteenth-floor service elevator, to meet Michael.

If he recognized me at all when the doors opened, he gave no outward indication. He pushed the cart out into the hall, handed me a white jacket and pressed the down button. His blank gaze regarded me balefully until it was cut off by the closing doors.

I put on the jacket and experimented with the cart until I got the hang of the wheels, finally wheeling it to the door of room 1511.

"Who?" a gruff voice demanded from within in answer to my knock.

"Room service," I called out, almost choking as the cotten wads came loose in my mouth, threatening to tumble down my throat. I stuffed them firmly against my cheeks just before the door swung inward.

"Come," the man who answered the door ordered. He looked like someone who was accustomed to being obeyed. He was a little taller than me, dark-haired, trim and neat. I couldn't imagine this man ever having so much as one hair out of place.

He shut the door behind me and said, "Search him." A second man, who had been off to one side, approached me and began to expertly pat me down. He wouldn't find anything. I had left Wilhelmina, Hugo and Pierre behind in my suitcase. I felt totally naked and vulnerable without them; but leaving them behind had been necessary, in order to avoid any possibility of a confrontation with the Russians.

The man searching me stepped back and stood at ease. He was bigger than the first man, younger, obviously the muscle of the two, but also obviously a subordinate.

That left the lady with the hatchet face.

At that moment a door opened and she stepped through it. I could see why Angel had made several such references to her. It was really the only way to describe her. Aside from that, she was about five-foot-one, blade thin, somewhere in her fifties.

"What is this?" she demanded of the neat man who'd opened the door for me. I no longer had any doubt of who was in charge of Belnikov's security. Her English was heavily accented, and it seemed to pain her to have to use the foreign language.

"Breakfast," I told her, before the man could speak. The cotton wads in my mouth did wonders for my voice. I didn't even recognize it as my own. Her eyes flicked to me momentarily, then away, dismissing me as being of any importance.

"Well," she said, without looking back at me, "leave it."

"You must sign, Miss," I said, trying to sound as if English were not my native tongue, either.

She motioned to me impatiently and I stepped toward her and handed her the check. At that point the door she had come through opened again and a man I assumed was Belnikov entered the room. Hawk hadn't been able to show me a photo, because he said that none existed.

This man was tall and painfully thin—he looked like a man who had died long ago, and was just looking for a comfortable place to lie down. He had high cheekbones which threatened to burst through pale, paper-thin skin. His hands, long-fingered and dry-skinned, reached out toward the woman as he asked, "Is that my breakfast?" His English was almost without discernible accent.

"Yes, Comrade Belnikov," she answered.

"I will sign," he told her.

"Comrade—"

"Major, I am perfectly capable of signing my own name," he insisted, wiggling his long, thin fingers at her.

She compressed her lips tightly for a moment, then said, "As you wish, Comrade Belnikov," and handed him the check.

"I need a pen," he said aloud, to no one in particular. I stepped forward and handed him mine, sorry that I hadn't thought up some way to write the recognition sign on it.

"Thank you," he said, taking it from me.

"A pleasure, Comrade Belnikov," I told him. "I am a great admirer of yours. It is a pleasure to meet you."

"You play chess?" he asked.

"I dabble," I answered, trying to sound modest and nervous.

"We all dabble, young man," he told me sagely, handing back the check and the pen.

"I have memorized many of your famous moves," I told him.

"Really?" He wasn't the least bit interested.

"Yes, especially Knight to King Bishop Six, where

you forked your opponent's King and Queen and eventually left him with no alternative but to resign."

If he recognized the sign he didn't let it show on his face. I could see by his eyes, though, that he was looking a bit closer at me.

At that point no one in the room was able to see my face but him, so I made an effort to negate the effect of the cotten wads by shifting them in my mouth, but I had the feeling that I simply looked like I was making obscene faces at him. I hoped that, to some extent, he was able to see the man behind the disguise. I hoped that the next time he saw me he would be able to make the connection.

"Please," the lady major said, touching my arm.

I popped the wads back into place and turned to face her. "I'm sorry," I told her. "I will come back for the cart later."

"That will be fine," she told me.

"Thank you," Belnikov said.

"You are welcome, sir. Again, it was a great pleasure to meet you at last."

"Major," he snapped, "show the gentleman our appreciation for the swift service."

Again she looked annoyed, but she gestured to the neat looking man and he dug into his pocket for my tip. He sorted the bills in his pocket and handed me the Swiss equivalent of a dollar bill. He actually smiled when he handed it to me.

I stared at it for a moment, then put it into my pocket and said, "Thank you," and was ushered from the room by the bigger man.

When I reached the staircase, I removed the cotton and the mustache, combed my hair out with my fingers and draped the waiter's jacket over my arm.

I had finally made contact—of a sort—and it was time to communicate with Hawk.

SEVENTEEN

"Do you think he saw the real you?" Hawk asked from my hotel television set. I had modified it, using material from the false bottom of my suitcase. I had just finished recounting the events up to the present time, minus a detail or two.

"I can only hope so, sir. At least we know that he acknowledged the recognition sign."

"You're sure of that?"

"He's the best chess player in the world," I told Hawk. "He's got to have a quick mind to have gotten where he is."

"You're not sure."

I turned my head and made a face, then turned back. "Reasonably certain, sir."

"No problems such as the one you had in Atlantic City?" he asked.

"Just one," I told him. I went over the story of being shot at in the snow. "I dug the slug out; it was a .38."

"The same caliber as the one you saw in Mr. Leonard's room," he observed. No one had ever accused Hawk of not listening.

"Right."

"I assume you've checked his room?"

"Not yet, just the same drawer. I have checked the file you gave me, though," I said, showing him the folder. I had read it through again before contacting him.

"There's nothing here to indicate any reason why he should be carrying a gun. There's also nothing here to indicate that he is anything other than what he seems to be." I dropped the folder and added, "He has been hitting the bottle at a heavy clip, though."

"That makes him dangerous," Hawk observed.

"I agree, sir."

"Very well, N3. Proceed with caution, and let me know when you are ready for the plane."

"When I get things set up to get him off this mountain, I'll let you know," I promised, then broke the contact, and his nodding face vanished.

I took Leonard's folder and dropped it into my suitcase with the others. I had taken all the folders Hawk had prepared for me on the Atlantic City trip, and now I had separated them. There were only a half a dozen people here in Switzerland who had also been in Atlantic City: Leonard, Nikki, myself and three others.

I took Nikki's folder out and leafed through it again. When she wasn't playing chess she was a fashion coordinator for a large department store chain. Preliminary workup on her revealed nothing unusual, as in Leonard's case.

The other three repeaters from Atlantic City were men. The three of them were familiar names in the chess field: Aiello, Ciccarelli and Wargo. All three men had been on the "chess circuit" for at least ten years.

Had one them engineered the two attempts already made on my life?

They were the only common denominator in the two attempts, which had taken place thousands of miles apart. That made them all suspect.

As well as watching out for Belnikov, I was going to have to keep an eye on those five people. One good thing was Belnikov's security. It should be good enough to keep him safe from harm until I could get him away.

The bad thing was, the security was probably also tight enough to make that very difficult.

For something to do, I read through the folders again, then checked my watch. It was almost time for the first match of the day. I put everything back in my suitcase and went down to put in an appearance.

Both opponents were present when I arrived, and a good number of the other competitors had arrived to watch the match. When this one was over, there were others scheduled to go on simultaneously. We were waiting for the Tournament Director to arrive to act as Match Referee; he would make certain that all of the laws of chess would be followed. The match would not start until he declared it so.

"When this is all over," a voice said from behind me, "we should have ourselves a new champion."

I turned to find Martin Leonard, the inevitable drink in hand, approaching me.

"You think Belnikov's ready to be taken?" I asked him.

"I think I'm ready to take him," he replied. "I won't make any mistakes, this time."

"You're already making one, Martin."

"This?" he asked, raising the glass in his hand. "This is just a pick-me-up. Once the first match starts, I won't take another drink. You'll see, Nick. Just wait, you'll see."

He strolled away. I wondered if even he believed everything he'd just said.

I felt someone tap me on the shoulder firmly, and turned again, this time to find Nikki standing behind me.

"Why didn't you stay for breakfast?" she asked, trying to appear hurt. "I missed you when I woke up."

"I had a delivery to make," I told her.

"What?"

The Match Referee arrived and I used his arrival to

avoid Nikki's questions. "The match is about to start," I told her. "Can I get you a cup of coffee?"

She looked at me suspiciously and answered, "Sure, why not?"

When I returned, the match had just gotten underway. One of the competitors was Gerry Aiello, one of the men who had been in Atlantic City. The youthful appearance of his face belied the fact that his hair was thinning. He was only, according to my folder, thirty-five and had been playing competitively for twelve years. He had been young when he started, but had never been touted as a "boy wonder" the way Martin Leonard had. He hadn't had to face that kind of pressure early in his career, so his game had progressed unimpeded. Right from the outset, he seemed to outclass his opponent, and it was soon apparent who the winner would be.

When his opponent resigned there was a light smattering of applause, and he accepted the congratulations of some of his peers.

I left Nikki and approached Aiello with my hand outstretched. "Congratulations," I told him, pumping his hand.

He stared at me, blankly. Either he had no recollection of who I was—or he wanted me to think he didn't.

"Have we met?" he asked.

"I'm sorry, I thought you might remember," I said. "My name is Nick Crane. I was in Atlantic City—"

"Oh, right, right, of course. How are you?" he asked, pumping my hand now. By all appearances, he was being polite, still with no idea of who I was.

"Fine. Just wanted to compliment you on a well-played game," I told him.

"Well, thanks. Good luck with your first match."

"Thanks."

He walked off and I turned to look for Nikki, only she was gone. Maybe I'd hurt her feelings. Well, that was okay for now. I didn't need her hanging on my arm at the moment.

I walked out by the front desk and Angel waved me over.

"Hi," I said.

"Good morning. Michael is worried about his jacket?"

"Was that his? I thought it was a little big."

"Is it okay?"

"It's spotless; I've got it in my room. He'll get it back, I promise."

"Okay. Did you meet the great man?"

"I did, thanks to you."

"Don't mention it. You looking for your lady friend, Miss Barnes?"

"No, why?"

She leaned on the desk top and said, "Oh, I just thought you might want to know where she went."

"Where'd she go?"

"She came storming through the lobby here like she had something on her mind, and she met a man. They went up in the elevator together."

I thought about that a moment, then realized that it really didn't matter much to me one way or the other. "So?"

"So, I thought you might be interested in knowing who the man was."

"Okay, I'll bite."

"One of the guys who arrived with your friend, last night."

"My friend?"

"Yeah, the Russian, Belnikov."

"Which one?" I asked, suddenly very interested.

"The smaller, better looking one. You know, the neat one."

Nikki and one of the Russians.

Very interesting.

EIGHTEEN

I thanked Angel for the information and went to the lounge to ponder it. I ordered a bourbon and drank it sitting alone at the bar. Behind me some of the competitors had grabbed a few booths and were busily discussing the first match of the competition.

I had something else to occupy my mind: *Nikki and the neat Russian.*

Could I allow something simple like Nikki meeting a man in the lobby of a hotel to project her into the number one spot on my list of "people not to trust"?

I dropped some money on the bar and decided to check it out. I would go up to Nikki's room and knock on the door. If she and the man were there, I'd apologize and back off. If there was no answer, I was going into the room to take a look around.

Of course, if she didn't answer the door, that didn't necessarily mean that they weren't inside.

That was a chance I'd have to take.

I did everything but pound on her door, and there was still no answer. Using some special tools I was able to get inside her room without the proper key. The chessboard that we had used the night before was still on the floor. I walked quietly to the bedroom door and listened for tell-tale sounds from within. Hearing none, I ventured forth and pushed the door open.

The room was empty.

I did a thorough job of searching her room but found nothing out of the ordinary. She must have been in Belnikov's room at that moment.

I went up to room 1511 and knocked on the door. I decided to play it straight, just one competitor welcoming another.

The bigger Russian man answered the door.

"I'd like to see Mr. Belnikov," I told him, hoping that I appeared totally innocent, and also that he wouldn't remember me as the bellboy from that morning.

"Impossible," he said, and started to close the door. I put my foot in the way and he looked down at it, then stared at my face.

"There's really no need to be rude," I told him. "I simply wish to welcome Mr. Belnikov to the competition. My name is—" I began, but he didn't wait for me to finish.

He put a massive hand against my chest and pushed, propelling me backwards and into the wall opposite the door. The impact knocked the breath from my lungs. The damage was really not all that severe, but I tried to make it seem like it was. I expected him to simply shut the door from the inside, but he didn't. He stepped out into the hall, and then I knew what I was up against.

He was big, he wasn't all that intelligent, and he only knew how to go in one direction at a time. The push had set the direction, and he didn't know how to back up after it. He only knew to step forward and follow it up. I was faced with a dilemma.

In order to appear to be just another chess player, I'd have to let him knock me around at will and stop when he felt like it. The only problem with that was that he might not stop until I was dead, or damned near it.

If I mixed it up with him and came out on top, the Russians would then have to suspect me of being more than what I claimed to be.

I had to avoid getting hurt too badly and at the same time avoid hurting the big man. It was hard to avoid hurting someone, however, when he had no such intention toward you.

I stayed slumped against the wall as he approached me, then as he lunged I let myself fall to the floor. At the same time I kicked out, hoping it would look accidental. I caught him on the shin and that, coupled with his own lunge, caused him to fall, hitting his head on the wall above me. I rolled out of the way just in time to keep him from falling on me. I staggered to my feet just as the hatchet-faced woman came to the door.

"Boris!" she shouted at the big man, but he was down on all fours, shaking his head, trying to clear it.

"I'm—I'm sorry," I told her, stammering purposely. "I didn't mean to—to hurt him. I was just trying to get out of his way."

I maneuvered so I'd be able to look into the room and was surprised by what I saw.

Nikki was there, holding a glass of champagne; Belnikov was standing next to her. The neat Russian man was not in sight. Both Nikki and Belnikov were trying to look past the major to see what was happening. When Nikki saw me she looked surprised.

"Boris, get up," the major told the big man, ignoring me.

"Let me help," I said, grabbing one of Boris's massive arms.

I assisted him to his feet, which were still unsteady beneath him, but his direction was unchanged. As clouded as his thinking was at the moment, he only had one thing in mind.

"Boris," she called out, then said something very swiftly in Russian. I caught the gist of it, which was for him to stop. He looked at her balefully, then seemed to relax. He continued to shake his head, though. There was a massive lump forming on his forehead, and it was starting to turn colors.

"You will leave," the major said to me, making damned sure I knew that it was an order.

"Now wait just a minute," I protested. "I'm an American citizen—"

"Major," Belnikov called from the room.

She compressed her lips, displaying her annoyance, then turned and said, "Comrade Belnikov?"

"Show Mr. Crane in, please."

"Comrade—"

"Show him in, major," Belnikov said in a sterner tone.

She looked at me with fire in her eyes, then stepped back and said, "Come in."

"Thank you," I told her, squeezing past her. Boris entered behind me and she shut the door.

"You had better put some ice on that," I told Boris, and when he didn't answer I turned to Belnikov. "I'm really sorry about this, Comrade Belnikov."

"A mistake, Mr. Crane. Do not apologize," he told me. "Would you like some champagne?"

"Please. What is the occasion?"

"Ah," he said, handing me a glass and then filling it, "I have been wanting to meet Miss Barnes for some time. I have heard that she is the finest female chess player in the world. I sent one of my companions down to ask her to join me this afternoon for lunch. We have already ordered, but if you like—"

"That's quite all right," I assured him. "I have no wish to intrude, I only wanted to meet you."

"And so you have," he told me. His eyes were studying my face closely, but I decided against giving him the recognition sign once again. I felt fairly confident that he had recognized me, and that was all I needed to know. To some extent, he had also vindicated Nikki. Her meeting with the neat Russian—who was conspicuously absent—was logically explained away.

I finished the champagne and set the glass down. "I'll be going and allow you two to continue getting acquainted," I told him. I extended my hand to him and added, "Perhaps you can find some time for us to have a chat."

"I will endeavor to do so, I assure you. I apologize for the difficulty you have just experienced."

I shook my head and said, "It's better forgotten. Thank you for the champagne."

"It was my pleasure."

"Nikki, see you later," I said, speaking to her for the first time. She raised her glass to me and smiled.

"Major, would you see Mr. Crane out, please?" Belnikov said to the woman. It was not a request.

"As you wish, Comrade," she replied. She led me to the door, opened it, then slammed it shut before I could thank her.

NINETEEN

Nikki was not totally in the clear, but she had come back to the pack considerably. As for Belnikov, as far as I was concerned, positive contact had been made. All that was left for me to do now was to watch and wait for the opening I needed to whisk him away.

As I entered the elevator I realized that I had completely forgotten about my own match with Martine. A check of my watch showed that it was scheduled to start in ten minutes.

I needn't have rushed, however, because Martine herself did not arrive until considerably after the Match Referee. The move was no doubt designed to psych me out by making me wait. Unfortunately for the lovely Martine, she couldn't possibly hope to psych me out, because I didn't particularly care whether I won or not, whether it be the match, or the whole competition. For that reason, I was probably much more relaxed than any of the other players.

While waiting for Martine to show up, I wondered again where the other Russian had been during my visit to Belnikov's room. I kept coming up with the same answer: my room!

What would make them suspect me, though? Why would the lady major send him there, if not because my cover had been blown. Were they behind one or both of the attempts on my life?

I decided not to worry about it. I couldn't check my room until my match was over—and I couldn't start my match until Martine arrived, which she finally did, a half an hour late.

With muttered apologies to the referee and to me, she sat down and the match began, with her making the first move, playing white.

Concentration is essential when playing chess, especially on a tournament level. One of the major problems I'd had to overcome, under the tutelage of Evan Clarke, had been keeping a written record of every move I made, while playing. Each player was required to do so. I had had trouble keeping my concentration when I had to stop and write down every move. It had taken me a while to overcome the problem and eventually it had ceased to *be* a problem and simply became the minor annoyance it was to all players.

Martine had to be a little upset that her sexual ploy had failed without even a nibble. It was obvious that she did feel I was a threat, otherwise she would not have used the ploy of arriving late.

She made her first mistake early, and I knew I would have no problem. She was too emotional a woman to be an excellent chess player. She had to be warned once by the referee for an outburst when she made an obvious blunder and became enraged at herself. Finally she was forced to resign and stalked from the room without the customary congratulations to the winner.

I accepted praise from my fellow competitors, but I knew that Martine had defeated herself before she had even sat down. I did not expect to be so lucky, next time.

Declining a victory drink, I hurried up to my room and took a look around. No matter how well it may have been searched, I'd be able to tell.

My door was locked when I reached it. I opened it

with my key and stepped in. I didn't even have to look around to know that someone had been there. I could feel it! The *air* was not the way I had left it. People have distinctive scents, even if they don't wear perfumes or colognes, and the scent in the room was different, foreign. There was no doubt about it, my room had been searched.

By whom? The Russians, or someone else?

I'd find out sooner or later, but for now, I would have to play it as if my cover had been blown.

TWENTY

Everything had been put back in its proper place, but I was still convinced that the room had been searched. I checked my electronic equipment in the false bottom of my suitcase, and it was all there, seemingly untouched.

I checked my watch. My match with Martine had been unusually quick, due to her own unforced errors; consequently there was still about ten minutes to go before Belnikov's scheduled match.

I decided to go down and catch it.

When I arrived Belnikov was already there in his seat. His three "companions" were all in attendance, and no more than a couple of arm lengths away. Also in attendance, among many others eager to see the champion at work, was Nikki. I stayed on the opposite side of the room from her and waved. She returned the wave, and smiled.

Belnikov's opponent was American, one of the men who had also been in Atlantic City, Lew Ciccarelli. Certainly an accomplished player, a thorough professional, no one really expected him to be a match for Belnikov.

The Match Referee signalled the match to begin, and Belnikov made his first move, advancing with a conventional Ruy Lopez. No one knew where he would go from there. Belnikov had the reputation of being the most unpredictable champion the chess world had ever seen.

Ciccarelli was clearly outclassed, but he did not make any unforced errors, as Martine Dupree had done, so he lasted much longer than she did. Almost an hour and a half later, he resigned, and shook Belnikov's hand.

The match over, Belnikov stood up and was immediately flanked by his "companions" and, to my surprise, by Nikki Barnes. They all marched to the elevator and went up to the fifteenth floor.

Other matches were beginning, but the main event was over and people began to file out of the room. I was suddenly reminded that I had not seen Martin Leonard for some time, not even in the bar, which was unusual.

Maybe he was passed out drunk somewhere.

I checked the bar, just to make sure, but he wasn't there. It wasn't so much that I was worried about him. When I'm on an assignment and something looks unnatural, that worries me. Martin Leonard not being in the bar, or at least in evidence, was unnatural. I decided to check his room.

His door was locked, and when I knocked there was no answer. I pounded on the door some more, and when there was still no answer I opened it the same way I had opened Nikki's.

As I entered the room and shut the door behind me, my instincts went to work. Things were not right in the room; I could feel it in the air again. It was different, though, this time. It was not just that someone had been there who didn't belong. There was a smell in the air that I had become quite familiar with over the years.

The smell of death.

I found him in the bathroom, stuffed into the tub. The blood led in dry tracks to the drain, dark brown and crusted. He'd been killed sometime the night before, shot in the head.

I hadn't touched anything in the room, and now I

used my handkerchief to close the bathroom door. I hated to do it, but I was going to leave the task of finding his body to the maid. This way I would simply be interviewed along with the rest of the competitors. If I reported finding his body, the police could tie me up for some time and I might miss my opportunity to take off with Belnikov in tow.

I checked the hallway to make sure no one was around before leaving the room, locking the door behind me. Instead of waiting for the elevator, I took the stairway down to my floor and entered my room.

I had not taken the time to search Leonard's room for fear that someone would find me, but I wondered if his gun was still there and if it was the weapon used to kill him.

Of course, the overriding question was, who killed him and why? What possible motive could someone have for killing an alcoholic chess player? It was pretty clear that he wouldn't have been killed by one of the competitors out of fear that he might win the competition. Everyone knew that Martin Leonard would always find some way to lose the big match, even if he made it to the finals.

If anything, he was self destructive. One way or another he would have found a way to destroy himself, had someone not already done it for him.

In my effort to figure out who would want him dead, I wondered if the Russians somehow decided that he was a danger? What if they hadn't fingered me as an American agent, but Martin Leonard instead?

That being the case, it could very well have been me lying in the bathtub with a bullet through my head.

And if the Russians realized their mistake, I could very well be next.

TWENTY–ONE

As had been the case in Atlantic City, I wanted to be among people when the body was finally discovered. I would also have to walk around weaponless for some time. I didn't want the police finding a gun on me while investigating a shooting death. Since my room had already been searched once, I saw no danger in leaving my arsenal behind. Nevertheless, I hid them as well as I could before going down to join the crowd that was watching the afternoon matches.

I stopped at the bar, got a bourbon and took it into the competition room with me. I made a point of striking up a conversation with three or four of the players who were watching, and was discussing end game strategy when the buzz began to filter through the crowd. I knew then that the body had been found.

"Did you hear?" a small man asked, approaching me.

"What?" I responded, curiously.

"The American, Martin Leonard. He was shot, right in his room!"

"Shot," a man beside me repeated.

"No!" I said, trying my best to sound shocked.

"I'm sorry," the little man said suddenly. "Was he a friend of yours? I did not mean to blurt—"

"No, no," I told him, "that's quite all right. I only

knew him slightly, from our last competition, but it's still a shock. He was my countryman, after all."

"True," the small man said, and hurried off to spread the news.

"This could be distracting," the man with me said.

"To say the least," I agreed. "The police will no doubt want to question us all."

"All?"

"Well, we all knew him, to some extent. He was part of the competition."

"I suppose you are right."

The players who were involved with their matches were casting displeased glances at the crowd as the volume in the room rose. The Match Referee asked for quiet and part of the crowd began to disperse and go into the bar, where they could continue their conversation concerning the news of Leonard's death.

I decided to play at being curious about the death of my fellow American, and went out to the desk to talk to Angel.

"Oh, Nick, it's terrible," she told me.

"What happened, Angel?"

"One of the maids went into Mr. Leonard's room to clean up. She actually cleaned most of the room without finding him, but when she went into the bathroom there he was, in the bathtub. There was so much blood the poor woman fainted. When she came to she began screaming."

"Have the local police been called?" I asked.

"Yes, they're on the way."

An idea began to form in my mind. I would have liked to be present as each member of the competition was being questioned, especially Belnikov.

"Angel, could you let me know as soon as they arrive? I'd like to speak to the officer in charge of the investigation."

She leaned forward and asked in a low voice, "Do you

know something about it, Nick?"

"No, but maybe I can help."

"How?"

I shrugged. "You never know. Will you do that for me?"

"Okay," she agreed.

"In fact, mention my name to them and tell them that I'd like to speak to them before they talk to anyone else."

"What's going on?"

"That's what they'll have to find out."

"No, I mean with you. You've been acting like you're here to do more than just play chess. Ever since you got here, you've been acting funny—" she went on, but I cut her off.

"Angel, you're a very curious person."

"Me?" she asked, surprised. "I was just thinking the exact same thing about you."

"Well, maybe if you're a good girl, you'll get some answers to your questions."

"I'm going to hold you to that, Nick."

"Okay. Let me know as soon as they get here."

I went back to my room and played with my television until I was looking at the craggy face of my boss, David Hawk. Briefly, I explained what had happened and what I wanted to do.

"Can you take care of that for me, fast?" I asked.

"It'll be done, N3. I think it's an excellent idea. It will enable you to know everything the police know, but how can you be sure they'll allow it?"

"American television is very popular in foreign countries. If I get a cop who watches a lot of it, that should influence him enough."

"Good luck, and be careful."

I dissolved David Hawk's countenance and returned the television to its original state.

I changed my clothes in an attempt to look less like a

chess player and more like a hardboiled American. It was essential to my proposed masquerade. I was just about done when the phone rang.

"Mr. Crane?" a man's voice asked.

"That's right."

"My name is Inspector Borga, Mr. Crane. I understand you have some information for me pertaining to the murder of your fellow countryman."

"That's not exactly right, Inspector, but I would like to speak to you before you question any of the other members of the chess tournament."

"I am in Mr. Leonard's room. Do you know where that is?"

He was playing cop already. "Yes, I do, Inspector. I'll be down in a couple of minutes, if that's all right?"

"That will be fine, Mr. Crane. I will be waiting."

I decided against making him wait any longer than just a couple of minutes and went right down.

"Nick Crane," I told the uniformed officer on the door.

"Go right in, sir."

The room was a flurry of activity. Police crime scenes are the same the world over, only the language changes. There are still flashing bulbs, fingerprint dust and lots of people standing around. In the center of all this hubbub sat a man, a bored looking man. The man in charge is always the most bored looking because he has the least to do.

I approached him, "Inspector Borga?"

"Mr. Crane. Have a seat, please."

I sat in a chair facing the couch and crossed my legs.

"If you please, Mr. Crane, I would appreciate it if you would get right to the point. I have much to do."

He was in his early forties, steel wool hair, gray eyes, a long jaw that needed a shave. He looked like a man who hadn't been to bed in days.

"It's very simple, Inspector. First of all, Martin

Leonard was a countryman of mine."

"Not a friend?"

I shook my head.

"An acquaintance, and a fellow competitor. That's the other thing. This competition means a lot to me and I don't want to see it ruined. I want to help you find the killer."

"Commendable."

"I want to offer you my assistance," I clarified. "You won't find me unfamiliar with homicide investigations."

"Oh, and why is that?"

"I'm a retired police officer, homicide detective from Washington, D.C."

"A detective?"

I didn't want to make him feel there was any competition.

"Just a detective, first grade. I wasn't quite bright enough to make lieutenant, but I knew my job."

The last remark had no effect on him. He digested what I had told him, then called over another man in plainclothes. They spoke briefly and then the other man went out of the room.

"Would you have a little time to wait, Mr. Crane?" he asked.

"Certainly."

As I had expected, they were checking out my story. I hoped that Hawk had time to arrange for my story to be confirmed by the D.C. police department.

While I was waiting they took Martin's body away in a plastic body bag. The crowd began to thin out as the photographer and lab men completed their jobs and left. Borga himself spent some time wandering around the hotel room, and an inordinate amount of time in the bathroom—not for conventional reasons. Maybe he just had a dried, crusted blood fixation.

Eventually, the man he had sent to check out my story returned and they had a huddled meeting in a corner, after which Borga came back and sat on the couch again. He continued our conversation as if we'd never suspended it.

"Your qualifications seem excellent, Mr. Crane, excellent indeed. Would you be wanting anything in return for your services? Money, eh, publicity—"

"No, Lieutenant, no money, no credit. Chess tournaments are part of my retirement. Someone has disrupted my retirement. I want him caught, so I can get back to playing chess with no outside interference."

"How would you propose we use you?"

"Well, I know some of the people you'll be talking to. I know some better than I know others. I thought perhaps I could sit in on the interviews, perhaps just give you my feelings about each of the people you talk to. I will remain quiet during the interviews, unless you request that I speak."

He listened to me intently, then nodding said, "Very well, Mr. Crane. I will welcome your expertise."

He signalled one of his men and the interviews began. The only ones present were Borga, myself and two of his plainclothes men.

They were done one at a time and, for the most part, only took five or ten minutes each.

Did you know the deceased? If yes, how well? When did you last see him? Did you like him? If not, why? Do you know of anyone who did dislike him? If so, why? Do you know of anyone who might have wished him any harm? If yes, who and why?

There weren't too many yes answers, so there weren't that many "whys" asked. Consequently, there were not that many interviews that went beyond five minutes.

There were a couple of interviews I was particularly interested in. The first was Nikki.

"Your name?"

Borga did all of the talking. There was never so much as a peep out of his two subordinates.

"Nikki Barnes."

"You are American?"

"Yes."

She was very curious as to why I was being allowed to sit in on her interview, but beyond a questioning look, there was nothing she could do.

"Were you acquainted with the deceased?"

"I was."

"How well did you know him?"

"Not well."

He smiled at her, but it didn't mean he was happy. Maybe he just thought she was pretty. Pretty girls are for smiling at.

"I'll rephrase the question. How long have you known, or been acquainted with, the deceased?"

"I've only seen him at one or two other tournaments. I don't think we ever really spoke more than ten words to each other."

"I see. Then you wouldn't know anyone who might want to kill him would you?"

She looked at me for a moment, then back at him and shook her head. "No."

"Was there anyone here at the competition that he was particularly friendly with?"

Again she looked at me and then shook her head. "Mr. Crane was the only person I really saw him spend any time with."

Borga looked at me with his eyebrows raised.

"I put him to bed once when he was drunk," I told him. "I'm sure you'll find some of my prints in the room, and I'm sure you can check the story with the bar and restaurant staff. After that, we had one or two drinks together, but I couldn't keep up."

"The victim drank heavily?"

I nodded. "If he wasn't already, he was on the verge of becoming an alcoholic."

He turned his attention back to Nikki.

"Did the victim ever, ah, make advances—"

She shook her head. "Never."

Borga seemed to sense something between Nikki and myself, because he turned to me and asked, "Do you have any questions for Miss Barnes?" He hadn't done that with any of the others.

I had a whole lot of questions for Miss Barnes, but none that I wanted to ask at the moment.

"No, none."

"Very well, Miss Barnes. You may go. Please make no attempts to leave the hotel until further notice."

She nodded, looked at me once, and then left.

"You and the lady are . . . acquainted with each other?"

"We were, for a while, but I seemed to have been aced out by an older man."

"I beg your pardon, 'aced out'?" he asked, confused.

"Replaced."

"Ah," he said, then instructed one of his men to bring the next person in.

The next one was Belnikov, and he came in with his three "companions."

"I would like the rest of you to wait outside," Borga told them.

"We cannot leave Comrade Belnikov alone," the little major told him.

"He will not be alone," the Inspector pointed out.

"Why do you allow the American to stay?" she demanded.

"He is assisting with the investigation."

"I will not leave Comrade Belnikov in the room with the American," she said, stubbornly.

"Miss—"

"Major!" she snapped. He was about to speak again when she cut him off again. "We could create an incident, Inspector."

He considered that. "I will allow one of you to stay," he proposed.

They all looked at each other. Belnikov kept staring straight ahead, as if the whole thing had nothing to do with him.

They made their decision.

"Very well," she agreed.

I expected her to be the one to stay, but she was the first to leave, followed by big Boris. The neat man, whose name I had yet to hear, stayed and stood behind Belnikov.

Belnikov fielded all the questions very well and replied with one word whenever possible.

The word was usually "no."

"Any questions, Mr. Crane?" Borga asked.

I shook my head.

"None."

"All right, Comrade Belnikov, you may go. Please don't leave the hotel for any reason until we've settled this matter."

"As you wish," he replied, which was the longest sentence he'd used.

The remainder of the interviews were uneventful and repetitive. When the last person was gone, Borga stretched his hands up over his head, then rubbed them over his face.

"I have not been to sleep in over forty-eight hours," he said to no one in particular.

"It's a rough life," I remarked.

"Your Mr. Leonard seems to have been a singularly unimportant man. He left no lasting impression on anyone save that he always seemed to have a drink in his hand. Was he an unhappy man?"

"Very," I answered. "His life did not seem to go the way he wanted it to, and he always found someone or something else to blame."

"Whose life goes as planned?" he asked. "And who else can be to blame but ourselves? I was going to be a lawyer, a defender of the oppressed. Now, some would say I am the oppressor."

I didn't have an answer to that, so I kept silent. I didn't want to get involved in a philosophical discussion with him.

"Have you any observations now that the interviews are done?" he asked.

"I'm afraid not, Inspector. For the most part, everyone seemed to be telling the truth."

"For the most part?"

I put both hands out in front of me in a pushing motion and said, "Just a figure of speech, I'm afraid."

"And what of your own involvement with the deceased?"

I hesitated a moment, as if collecting my thoughts, even though I knew exactly what I was going to tell him.

"Martin Leonard was a lonely man, Inspector. He seemed to want to be friends, but he tried too hard, especially when he was, uh, under the influence. I was perhaps more tolerant of him than many of the others. As I said previously, I took him to his room on my first day here, to keep him from making a complete fool of himself in the bar. Beyond that . . ." I let it trail off and spread my hands out in front of me.

"Did he offend anyone on that day?"

"In the bar?" I asked, then shook my head. "Most of them were amused. I can't say for sure how everyone felt, but no one seemed to be offended."

He nodded, then said something to his two men. They replied shortly and left the room.

He got up and said, "I will be leaving now. If you should happen to think of anything that might help, please call me." He handed me a business card. It wasn't in English, but I was able to read the telephone number.

I rose to leave with him.

As we waited for the elevator I asked, "Inspector, have you ever watched any American television shows?"

He stared at me with a puzzled look on his face and said, "No, I do not have time for the television."

I nodded.

"Why do you ask?" he asked as the elevator arrived.

"Oh, no reason. Just curious," I replied, stepping into the elevator ahead of him.

TWENTY-TWO

I called Nikki's room from mine, but there was no answer. I wanted to talk to her about what was happening between her and Belnikov. Obviously, there was something afoot between the two, but a romance? I couldn't see it, or maybe I didn't want to. I don't normally admit to having an ego, but that was a possibility.

As I hung up I was struck by a thought. I wondered if Borga or his men had found Leonard's gun in the room. Would he have mentioned it to me if he had? Probably not, we hadn't actually discussed all of the aspects of the case. He'd simply agreed to let me sit in on the interviews.

I could have called and asked him, but then he would have wanted to know how I knew that Leonard had a gun. No, the best way would be to search the room again.

I took the elevator to Martin's floor and, as I stepped out of the elevator, saw that Borga had stationed a uniformed man at the door.

A second look told me I was in luck. It was the same man who had originally admitted me.

I approached him, smiling, and he watched me with a stony, no-nonsense expression on his face.

"Do you speak English?" I asked him.

"Yes."

"Good. Do you remember me?"

"Of course. You are the American detective who is assisting the inspector with the homicide investigation."

"Very good."

He was young and, apparently, eager to show his worth. He'd already successfully displayed his masterly command of English, as well as an excellent memory.

"You're English is very good," I said, stroking his ego a bit. "And your memory. I can see you are destined for more than just standing guard over crime scenes."

He straightened up and said, "Yes, sir. I go to school nights, to learn the psy—" he stumbled momentarily over the difficult English word, then successfully pronounced it "—psychology behind the criminal mind. I will soon be the youngest inspector in my department."

"I can see that. I wonder—" I began, then shook my head.

"You wonder what, sir?"

"Well, I was just thinking—I had told the inspector that, should I be instrumental in catching the criminal, I did not want any credit. However, if I am successful, why shouldn't someone get the credit, someone who deserves a break. Do you know what I mean?"

He was frowning at me, so I went ahead and made my meaning clearer.

"If you were to let me back into the apartment, to snoop around a bit, and I came up with something vital, we could tell the inspector that it was you who discovered whatever it is I might discover. That would help your career along, wouldn't it?"

He brightened. "Yes, sir." Then he frowned and asked, "But why would you—"

"Officer, what's your name?"

"Hanz," he said, and I didn't know if it was his first name or his last, but that didn't matter.

"Hanz, I will be leaving the country very soon," I

pointed out. "You, on the other hand, live here. What good would the credit do me? I will be gone. Therefore, it is only fitting that it should fall to you."

"That is very kind," he observed.

"Now, one thing that always used to help me in a homicide investigation was just being at the scene. You know, nosing around a little bit."

"Nosing around," he repeated, to show me he understood, when in all probability, he did not.

"If you could just unlock the door—"

He turned as if he were going to do just that, then stopped and looked back at me. "I really should check with the inspector," he said.

"That's true, you should. However, I've always found initiative to be an important quality for advancement."

"Initiative?"

"The ability to make a decision on your own, without guidance," I clarified.

He took a moment to consider it, then nodded his head and proceeded to unlock the door.

"I will let you know as soon as I find something," I assured him, entering the room.

He nodded eagerly, then shut the door behind me and locked it.

The fingerprint powder had made a mess of the hotel furniture. The maids would have a fit trying to get it all clean. Strewn about the floor here and there were several flashcubes that had been left behind.

I started checking the dresser drawers, then the night table drawer. No gun. Leonard's suitcase was still there, open. I rummaged through it, but found nothing. I walked into the bathroom and stared at the brown stains in the bathtub. Ignoring them, I opened the medicine chest, then checked the wastebasket. Still nothing.

I made a complete sweep of the rest of the room, checking under the couch cushions, and even removing the rear of the television. The gun was not in the apartment. Either he had gotten rid of it, or whoever killed him had taken it with them when they left? But why? Just to confuse the police as to the murder weapon?

I wondered if I could get Borga to show me the slug once it was dug out of Leonard's body. I was curious whether it would match the one I had dug out of the snow after it was fired at me.

Sitting down on the couch, I reviewed the interviews with Belnikov and Nikki. Theirs were the only ones that really were any different from the rest. Belnikov was too reticent during his, answering in one or two words, unless that was just the man's personality or reaction to authority, and I was reading something else into it. Nikki, on the other hand, had seemed too willing to mention my name when asked if Leonard had any friends among the other competitors.

I tried to think of something I had specifically said or done that might have changed her attitude toward me. If there was something, it was something I had said or done without realizing it. I was anxious to talk to her, for that reason and also for what she might be able to tell me about Belnikov.

Maybe, if she and Belnikov were getting cozy, I could use her to get messages to him. Those three "companions" of his never left his side for a moment; there were always one or two of them with him.

Where had the unnamed, neat man been when I was up in his room? I had assumed that he was searching my room, but perhaps I was wrong. Not about my room being searched, but about who had done it.

I suddenly realized that not everyone at the competition had been questioned. Belnikov had, but the three people with him had not. An oversight on Borga's part —and mine. Among the three of them there might have been a particularly revealing session.

I wondered if I could get any of the three to talk to me without Borga present. It was worth a shot.

Unlocking the door to the room from inside, I peeked out. Looking past the officer I could see that the hall was empty, so I stepped out. He looked at me hopefully.

"You found something?" he asked, eagerly.

"Perhaps," I told him, appearing pensive. "I have to think it over, however, before I decide. I'm going to get some dinner while I consider it. Can I have something sent up to you?"

He was momentarily disappointed, but the mention of food seemed to perk him up some.

"I am rather hungry," he admitted.

"Okay, Hanz, I'll have something nice and hot sent up from the kitchen."

"Thank you."

"I will let you know as soon as I decide if we have something or not, but remember, we did try and that is important, also."

"I will remember, Mr. Crane. Thank you."

I shook my head and said, "That memory. Good night, Hanz."

"Good night, Mr. Crane."

I stepped into the elevator and when the doors closed I murmured, "Jesus, what a dummy."

TWENTY-THREE

When I reached the lobby Angel was on the desk. I couldn't really remember a time when she wasn't.

"Don't you ever rest?" I asked her.

"What a short memory we have," she remarked, smirking.

"Touché. Listen, can you do me favor?"

"The man's insatiable," she remarked, looking toward the ceiling. Then added, "for favors, I mean."

"That's true. There's a cop on the door to Martin Leonard's room. Could we get some food sent up to him?"

"On the cuff?"

"Don't they do that here?"

She shrugged. "I don't know."

"Well, if you can't, then put it on my bill."

"Okay," she agreed, picking up the phone. "You going to have some dinner now?" she asked.

"I thought I might."

"Where's your friend, Miss Barnes?"

I shrugged. "You got me."

"That was kind of what I had in mind," she admitted. "Want some company?"

"Sure."

"Let me take care of this for you and then I'll meet

you inside. Why don't you order for both of us?"

"Okay. See you in a second."

I went into the restaurant and grabbed a booth, told the waiter to bring me a bourbon and a menu. I picked out something I thought was chicken and had the waiter translate it for me. In English it sounded fine, so I ordered two, and a crême de ménthe for Angel.

When Angel arrived she slid into the booth and said, "It's done. He'll be the most well-fed cop in town."

"Good. He was very helpful to me."

"Oh, how?"

"How's your drink?"

She shook her head and said, "Huh-uh, you're not going to shake me off that easy. Something's going on and I'm just too curious to stay in the dark any longer."

"Angel—"

"I'll make you a deal," she proposed.

"What kind of a deal?"

"A trade. I'll give you some information, and then you tell me what's going on. Deal?"

"What kind of information?"

"First tell me if it's a deal."

"It depends on the information. If I feel it's worth it, then we have a deal."

She regarded me for a moment, then said, "Okay, if that's the best we can do."

"It is."

"Well, for one thing, your lady friend seems to have had a change of heart about you. Not only did she have lunch with the Russian, but he just called down and ordered dinner for two—and I know he's not making it with Major Hatchet-face."

"I'd agree with that. Yeah, I guess it looks like I have been replaced," I agreed.

"If it's any comfort to you," she said, leaning forward, "I think she's nuts."

I took her hand and said, "Thanks, that soothes my ego."

She smiled and slapped the back of my hand.

"Then again," I added, "you're not interested in chess. Belnikov is supposed to be the greatest chess player in the world. Nikki Barnes is considered by some to be the best female player."

"You think the two of them are up there playing chess?"

"I may not go that far, but it might be a logical occurrence for them to be attracted to each other."

The waiter came with dinner and set our plates down in front of us. When he was gone she asked, "Do you think maybe she intends to use him to further her career?"

"That's also a possibility," I agreed.

"That must be it," she decided, cutting into her chicken. "After all, he's twice her age . . . although she's no spring chicken herself."

We ate in silence for a few moments, then she said, "Well, how about it?"

"How about what?"

"Our deal. You're not going to welch, are you?"

"That was your information? That I was being replaced by an older man? That was hardly earth shaking, Angel."

She regarded me shrewdly and said, "I knew you'd say that. I saved my bombshell for last."

"And that is?"

"Last night Martin Leonard placed a long distance call to the United States."

That got my attention. "To whom?"

"That's just it. There was some trouble making the connection, and the operator told him she'd call back when she made the connection."

"Did she?"

"Yes, but when we rang his room there was no answer. We tried several times after that, but never got an
answer."

"Angel, if we don't know who he was calling, do we
know where?"

"Yes. Washington, D.C."

TWENTY-FOUR

Why would Martin Leonard be calling a Washington, D.C. phone number when his file indicated that he lived in California?

"Angel, could you get me the number that he was calling?"

"I guess so, but it won't be easy. I'd have to find the same overseas operator that he spoke to for assistance."

"Will you try it for me?"

"Sure but, uh, could I finish my dinner first?"

"Of course. Go ahead, finish your dinner in peace," I told her.

"What about our deal?" she asked around a forkful.

"Let me think about it?" I told her.

"Oh, Nick Crane, you are the most exasperating man I've ever met."

"I'm working on it," I assured her.

As we finished our meal, I went over this new piece of information. It could have been very innocent, the call to D.C. Somebody he knew, some family member. I'd have to have Hawk check it out, see if Leonard had any family and, if so, where they lived.

If it wasn't family or friend, though, then who was it? Or was I just reading too much into the destination of the call being Washington, the center of political and international intrigue?

We decided against coffee or an after dinner drink, and Angel decided to go to her room to try and track down the telephone operator.

"Don't think that I forgot about our deal," she warned. "You're going to fork over your end, sooner or later." She got up and, as she was walking away said, just loud enough for me to hear, "Welcher."

I smiled and felt a little bad about taking advantage of her openness and good nature, but that passed. Using people was part of my business and if I let it start to bother me, I wouldn't be able to do my job properly.

It was getting late and the days' matches were over. The results were posted in the room set up for the competition for those who were interested. I was not, but I made a pass at it just for appearances. After that I went back to my room, took a shower and got comfortable. It was time to go over everything that had happened to date, from start to finish, and look for answers.

The most puzzling things I could come up with were Nikki suddenly making like an ornament for Belnikov's arm, and Martin Leonard's uncompleted phone call the night before his body was discovered. Did one or both have anything to do with the reason Belnikov and I were both in Switzerland?

His defection.

For that matter, did Leonard's death—his murder— have any connection? Coincidence is a bad word as far as I'm concerned. It isn't even in my vocabulary under normal circumstances. It's only when I'm denouncing it that I even think of it.

There was a connection here and I either had to find it or simply get around it by getting Belnikov out as soon as possible.

Maybe I could even get Nikki to help me do it, but that meant I had to get her away from Belnikov and his crew long enough to talk to her.

TWENTY-FIVE

I filed everything away in a small corner of my mind where I would subconsciously continue trying to fit the pieces together while I slept, without having them affect my sleep.

The next morning I awoke feeling refreshed and ordered breakfast in my room. I took all those pieces out from that corner of my mind and set them out on the table in front of me, but there were still a few missing. The first thing on my agenda for the new day was to get a hold of Nikki and see if she had any of the ones I was missing.

I called her room after breakfast, but there was no answer. After that, I tried the desk, hoping Angel was on duty, but was informed that she wouldn't be for a couple of hours. When I asked for her room number, I was told that they couldn't give that information out.

The day was not starting out on a high note.

Dressing, I remembered a question I had forgotten to add to the list last night: Where was Martin Leonard's gun?

I got out the card Inspector Borga had given me the day before and dialed his number. I had to speak to two other people before he finally came on the line.

"Have you obtained some information on the case,

Mr. Crane?" he asked.

"Not yet, Inspector. Nor have I formulated any theories yet. I would like some additional information, however."

"Such as?"

"What kind of gun was Leonard killed with?"

"Hold on a moment, I'll check the autopsy report. I've only just received it."

I heard him shuffling papers about, then silence when he must have found the proper page. "He was killed with one shot from a thirty-eight caliber pistol. Have you any information about such a gun?"

"I'm afraid not," I lied, "but I'll let you know if I find something."

"I see. Is that all you called for?" The inspector's tone clearly indicated that he had not considered me to be of much assistance in this matter.

"I'm afraid that was all, Inspector. Sorry."

"I must get back to work," he said abruptly, and hung up.

One good thing had come out of the conversation, if nothing else. Apparently the good Officer Hanz had not said anything to the inspector about my visit to the victim's hotel room. I could deal with the inspector's disappointment, but I was not particularly keen about trying to handle his anger.

One thing I didn't need was to be deported before I had a chance to arrange Belnikov's defection. Interfering with a homicide investigation in a foreign country would be all they would need to deport me.

I called Nikki's room again, still no answer. I was tempted to call Belnikov's room and ask for her, but decided against it. Instead, I went down to the restaurant and grabbed a table from which I could watch the desk. Three cups of coffee later Angel finally came on duty.

"Good morning," I greeted, approaching the desk.

"Oh, Nick. I just called your room."

"What's the good word?"

She shrugged helplessly. "I'm having trouble locating that particular operator, but I'll keep trying."

I didn't bother hiding my disappointment, but said, "Thanks anyway."

"What are you going to do this morning?"

"I'm trying to locate Nikki Barnes, but there's no answer in her room."

"That's no surprise. I saw her leaving earlier."

"She checked out?"

"No. Apparently she was going into town. She had the desk call her a cab."

"Who was on the desk?"

"Jules."

"Could you find out from him who he called?"

She shook her head. "I don't have to. We always call the same company."

"Great. Could you call them and find out where the cab took her?" I asked, aware that my favors were piling up and I still hadn't given her what she wanted.

"Wait a sec," she said, and picked up the phone. It took her about twenty minutes, but she finally hung up with the information.

"He took her into town."

"Where?"

She shrugged. "He dropped her off and left. He didn't see where she went."

"Great. I could start for town and she'd be on her way back."

"Not necessarily. She asked that the driver pick her up at one o'clock. That gives you about three-and-a-half hours."

I looked at my watch and saw that she was right. Nikki would have to be back for an afternoon match, according to the schedule. I didn't have a match until five.

"Can you get me a cab, Angel?"

"I already did. It's on the way. Same driver, too."

I kissed her on the cheek. "You're a gem."

"Sure. There's one other thing you should know, though."

"What's that?" I asked, already planning what I was going to talk to Nikki about once I found her in town, away from the Russians.

"She didn't go alone," she told me.

"Belnikov went with her?"

"No, but one of the Russians did."

"Which one?"

"The big one, Boris."

Wonderful! Now all I had to do was get to town, find Nikki, isolate her from Boris without arousing his suspicions—and hope she was willing to talk to me.

TWENTY-SIX

When the cab driver arrived at the hotel I had Angel explain to him just what I wanted him to do. It didn't come cheap, but we finally got him to agree to drop me off at the same spot he'd dropped Nikki and Boris off earlier. I also paid him to show up to pick them up a half hour later than they had arranged. That would give me an hour to separate her from Boris and talk to her.

My destination turned out to be more of a village than a city or a town. It was still large enough, however, for two people to miss each other unless at least one of them knew where to look.

Being in the village finally gave me the feeling that I was really in Switzerland. Inside of the hotel there was no particular indication of what country I was in, but now I was touched by some of the flavor, the quaintness, that was Switzerland.

With more than two hours to kill, I walked around a bit, looking in shop windows and watching the people go about their daily business. About twenty minutes later, I spotted a simple little restaurant and decided to have something to eat.

The place appeared to be a Mom and Pop operation, and the couple was very happy to have an American stop in. They had their teenage daughter—an alarmingly healthy looking girl of about eighteen—show me to a table and bring me some cold brew. They made suggestions as to what local dishes I should try and then, while they went off to prepare them, I asked if I could use the phone. They did not have a pay phone, but were only too happy to allow me to use theirs. I told them I was calling America, and would pay them for the use of the phone.

I would never have made the call from a hotel phone, which was why I always carried the equipment with me that enabled me to use a television or radio to make contact with Hawk. There was no way, however, that anyone could have assumed I would ever come into the village, stop at this particular restaurant and use the phone, so I considered it to be safe. Aside from that, the number I was calling in Washington *was* a safe number.

When I reached the overseas operator I asked her on a hunch if she remembered taking a similar call from the hotel a couple of nights before. She said she didn't, so I simply gave her the number that I wanted to call.

After several sign and countersign exercises, I finally got through to Hawk.

"I'm surprised that you are calling in, Nick," he said, careful not to use my code name although the phone was safe.

"So am I, sir, but circumstances dictated it. We have had a fatality here. The man we discussed in our earlier conversation."

"I see. Natural causes?"

"Decidedly not."

"I see," he said again.

"Did you come up with any new information on him?" I asked.

"Ah, nothing that I would like to discuss at the present time," he said, carefully.

That meant that he had found something else about Martin Leonard, something that might explain why he had a gun and why someone would want to kill him.

"I'll call again at a more opportune time, then, to find out what you have," I told him.

"That would be fine."

"Good-bye, then."

"Good-bye, Nick."

I hung up as the elderly couple came out with several plates of local delicacies. I forced the money for the call into the man's hands, and then sat down to sample the food. It was all delicious, and there was much more of it than I could ever hope to eat. The daughter stood to the side, watching me the whole time through large, brown eyes.

With only a short time left, I paid the couple for the food and hurried to the rendezvous point. I wanted to be there first, and be ready.

It took me about ten minutes before I found a little boy with whom I was able to communicate. For a few coins he agreed to deliver a message for me.

I was waiting about a half a block from the corner where the cab was going to meet them when, about five minutes before the appointed time, they finally showed up. Nikki was carrying a few boxes, and Boris was weighed down with twice the amount that she had. Apparently, the reason for the trip had been a shopping spree, no doubt financed by Comrade Belnikov.

I sent the boy into action and, as I had expected, he was totally ignored by big Boris. Nikki, on the other hand, bent down to talk to him and he whispered my message in her ear. I saw her eyes flick down the street momentarily, and I stepped out of the doorway I was in just long enough for her to see me.

Nikki waited a few moments, then leaned over and said something to Boris, who had to lean down to listen, much the way Nikki had to lean down to listen to the young boy. Boris listened intently, nodding his ponderous head, and then Nikki put down her packages and began to stroll down the block toward me, making it seem as if she were window shopping. When she reached the store whose doorway I was in she stopped and peered intently into the window.

"Come into the doorway, so he'll think you're going into the store," I instructed her.

She did so, and we both entered the store, which was a small curio shop.

"What is this all about?" she demanded.

"I just want to find out what I did wrong," I told her.

"What?"

I had decided to play it as if I were annoyed that she apparently had no intentions of seeing me any further. "Did I say something to offend you? I haven't been able to get you on the phone ever since you met Belnikov."

She looked down at her hands and said, "I'm sorry, Nick, but when I met Alexi, we just hit it off together, you know?"

"He's a lot older than you," I pointed out.

She looked disgusted and said, "That doesn't mean anything. He's kind and he's brilliant. I'm sorry it seems as if I'm just ignoring you, but he seemed to sense, that day you came up, that there was something between us. I-I wanted him to know that there wasn't anymore."

"Is he the jealous type?"

"Why?"

"I notice you never go anywhere without him, or without Boris."

"He's a very important man in his country. He's constantly in danger because of it, so they supply him with protection. He simply doesn't want anything to happen to me while I'm with him," she explained.

"I understand."

"I hope you do, Nick, I really hope you do." She touched my arm and looked into my eyes and said, "It was very nice," and I felt like somebody was pulling my chain.

"It was just so sudden," I told her, sounding like a bad B-grade movie.

She touched my cheek and said, "I know. I'm sorry."

"That's all right," I assured her, and she smiled.

"I wonder if you could do something for me," I said.

"What?"

"I'd like to, er, talk to Alexi without his entourage around. You think you could let him know?"

"I don't know if that can be arranged, Nick, but I'll tell him. It's the least I can do."

"Is he happy, Nikki?"

"Well, I hope so," she replied, misunderstanding what I meant.

"I don't mean that, I mean with his country, with the treatment he's getting."

She shrugged and said, "I imagine so, why?"

"Oh, I was just thinking what a treat it would be to have him living in the United States. You know, accessible, available to the rest of us mere mortal chess players."

She stared at me a moment, as if trying to find her voice, and then said, "You mean, defect?"

"I didn't mean—well, yeah, I guess I did mean that."

"Is that what you want to talk to him about, defecting?" she demanded.

"No, not at all. Don't get upset, Nikki. I mean, Jesus, what do you want to do, go back to Russia with him?"

She started to speak, then stopped and seemed to be thinking about what I said. "I really hadn't—"

"Or isn't it that serious?"

"It has been kind of sudden. It's not like it was with us. We both knew we'd be going our separate ways without even discussing it. Alexi and I, we really haven't—"

"Maybe you should," I suggested.

She looked at me and said, "I have to get back. Boris is probably waiting with the cab."

I touched her arm and said, "Think about it, Nikki, and don't forget to ask him to see me. Okay?"

"I have to go, Nick," she repeated, and left.

I waited a few minutes, then left and walked quickly the other way. The cab would take them back to the hotel, then return for me.

TWENTY-SEVEN

When I got back to the hotel Angel called me over to the desk.

"They just got back. Did you see her?" she asked.

"I saw her."

"Were you successful?"

"I don't know yet. It remains to be seen."

" 'It remains to be seen'," she mimicked. "You sound so damned mysterious."

"I don't mean to be, really," I told her.

"Yes, you do, but you'll pay," she told me, then turned away to take care of someone who wanted to register.

I couldn't tell if she was still kidding or not.

I went into what I had come to think of as the "game room" to check the schedule. Nikki had a match at two-thirty, and it was two-fifteen now. I wondered if the Russian entourage would come down with her. I toyed with the idea of going upstairs and getting in touch with Hawk again, but decided against it. I wanted to be there when she came down for her match, in case Belnikov came down with her.

Her opponent showed up on time, but Nikki was fifteen minutes late. Boris was with her, tagging along behind like a trained pup—a St. Bernard!

She gave her apologies to everyone and studiously avoided looking my way. Once the match began, all her concentration seemed to be on nothing else, and all Boris' attention was on her.

I decided to beard the lion in his den, to go up to Belnikov's room and try to get him to see me alone. I waved at Angel on my way to the elevator and she waved back, but without her customary smile.

At room 1511 I knocked on the door forcefully and the neat Russian man answered.

"Can I help you?" he asked.

"I'd like to speak to Comrade Belnikov," I told him.

Shaking his head he said, "I am afraid that you cannot—"

"Why don't we ask him?" I suggested.

"What is the problem, Vladimir?" the major asked from behind him.

"It is nothing," he told her. "Mr. Crane was just leaving."

"Mr. Crane?" she asked, peering around him, a look of distaste on her face.

"Hi," I said, waving.

"I have told you that you cannot see Comrade Belnikov," Vladimir told me. "Now please, go away."

The three of us were trying to speak at the same time now.

"Look, I just—" I began.

"Mr. Crane—" Vladimir said.

"You will leave at—" the major was ordering.

Suddenly, there was a loud noise from inside the suite, from the room beyond the front room. Belnikov's room, if I remembered correctly.

We all stopped and stared at each other. Vladimir was the first to move. I dashed past the major, right on his tail, and she brought up the rear. I saw him run into the door to the other room and bounce off.

"It is locked!" he shouted. He began to pound on it,

shouting, "Comrade, Belnikov!" in English, and then something else in Russian.

"Let's break it down," I proposed. He looked at me a moment, and then nodded, forgetting that just a few minutes ago he was trying to get rid of me. United by a common bond, we threw ourselves at the door and broke it open.

The first thing I noticed was Belnikov's absence from the room. He was nowhere in sight. The second thing I saw was the pieces of a broken vase on the floor.

"Belnikov!" I shouted.

"Where is he?" the major demanded, looking around.

There was another door against the left-hand wall, leading, I assumed, to the bathroom.

"What happened here?" Vladimir wondered out loud, standing over the pieces of the shattered vase.

I was afraid I knew, but I didn't say anything. I scanned the room quickly: the bed was unmade, there was a red-and-white chess set with a game going on, but nothing out of the ordinary. With the bathroom the only other room to check, I was afraid I knew just what we were going to find.

Vladimir and the major were acting very odd, very out of it, not at all like the professionals they were supposed to be. I left them where they were and went into the bathroom.

In life, Martin Leonard and Alexi Belnikov were in two different classes. In death, they had both ended up the same way, in a bathtub with their brains blown out.

TWENTY-EIGHT

"The Tub Killer," Inspector Borga said, disgustedly.

"What?" I asked, not sure I'd heard him right.

We were both standing in the bathroom, looking at Belnikov's body, folded up in the tub because he was so tall.

"That's what the newspapers are going to call him," he said, turning to look at me. "They enjoy creating nicknames."

"Call who?"

"The killer—whoever murdered Martin Leonard and Comrade Belnikov."

"You think it was the same person?" I asked.

"Don't you?"

I scratched my head and admitted, "It sure looks that way, doesn't it."

"It does. You think we are being misled?" he asked.

"I just don't think we should jump to any conclusions, Inspector, and I think you agree."

Having established a small bond between us, we left the bathroom together and went out to the front room. It was a flurry of activity, a duplicate of the scene in Leonard's room. On the couch sat the major and Vladimir. I couldn't understand their reaction to Belnikov's death. I expected them to be affected, sure, but not devastated. Maybe they had visions of Siberia dancing in their heads. After all, they had let a leading citizen of Russia be murdered right under their noses.

Right under my nose, too.

After finding Belnikov's body, I had immediately called Inspector Borga. I had expected an argument from the major and Vladimir, but after viewing the body they had turned curiously passive. I had practically led them to the couch and they hadn't moved since.

After calling Borga, I began to snoop around Belnikov's room. The only odd thing I found was a damp patch on the rug where the pieces of the vase had fallen. It was odd, because the flowers in the vase had been artificial. Why would the vase then have been filled with water?

I went back in to view the body after that. The body was lying in a fetal position, and the blood had begun to coagulate already, which I also found peculiar. It was too soon after we had first heard the commotion.

The only other thing I'd been able to establish before Borga's arrival was that all the windows in the room were locked from the inside, as had been the door that we broke down.

"How did the killer get out?" Borga said aloud as we left the room.

"I've been wondering about that myself."

"What about them?" he asked, indicating the two crestfallen Russians seated on the couch.

"I'm afraid I'm their alibi," I told him. "We were arguing at the door when we heard the vase fall."

"He must have been shot while you were trying to get into the room. None of you heard a shot?"

"No."

"I'm afraid I will have to question everyone once again."

"Maybe not. There are quite a few people down in the game room. Some competing, some watching. For instance, there's a man called Boris who was a member of the Russian party who is down there now, with Nikki Barnes."

"With Miss Barnes?"

"She's competing at the moment, which alibis her pretty well, doesn't it?"

"I suppose it does. Did she know the deceased?"

"They had begun getting along quite well over the last couple of days," I told him.

"I think I understand," he told me. "He is the older man who you said, ah, 'aced you out'?"

"He's the one."

"It is fortunate for you that you have an alibi, then," he told me.

I shook my head. "That wouldn't really have been a motive anyway, Inspector, believe me. Nikki Barnes and I were just *casual* friends," I told him, for want of a better word.

"No ego problem, Mr. Crane?"

"I wouldn't say I don't have something of an ego where women are concerned, but not in this case."

He observed me in silence for a few moments, then apparently decided to accept my word . . . for the moment, at least.

"I am going to question these two," he told me, indicating the people on the couch, "then send someone downstairs for Miss Barnes and this man Boris, whom you mentioned."

"Inspector, I wonder if you'd do me a favor?"

"What?"

"I'd like to go downstairs and break the news to Miss Barnes, if I may?"

He thought it over and agreed.

"I'll go down, but if she's not finished with her match, I'd rather wait until she is before I tell her. I promise I'll bring her up as soon as possible. That should give you time to talk to these two before she and Boris get here."

"Very well, Mr. Crane, but if it takes too long, I warn you, I will send an officer down to get all of you."

"Thank you," I said, and left.

In the elevator I tried to put things into proper perspective. My sole purpose for being here was to help Belnikov defect. Now that he was dead, I really had no reason to hang around. It wasn't my job to find out who killed him; that fell to Inspector Borga. However, I hated the thought of leaving something unfinished, and leaving without finding out who had murdered Belnikov went against the grain.

Then there was Martin Leonard's murder. Was it connected with Belnikov's, simply because both of their bodies were found in their bathtubs, shot through the head? But with the same gun?

As the elevator reached the main floor, I remembered that I wanted to contact Hawk to find out what he had discovered about Martin Leonard. But, I also knew that if I told Hawk that Belnikov was dead, he would probably order me to pull out.

For that reason, I decided that I would have to do without Hawk's additional information on Martin Leonard—at least for the moment.

TWENTY-NINE

Nikki's match was just about over. It was only a matter of her opponent realizing it, and resigning. Once he did so, she rose and was joined by Boris, who began to clear a path for her to the elevator. I intercepted them.

"Nikki—"

"Please, Nick, not now," she said, trying to get past me. I grabbed her arm, and Boris, in turn, grabbed mine.

"I've got something very important to tell both of you," I insisted. "Please listen. It'll be easier this way."

"*What* will be easier?" she asked, frowning. "What's wrong, Nick?"

"It's Belnikov," I said. I was about to go on when Boris suddenly jerked me around and almost shouted in my face.

"What has happened?" he demanded. His violent reaction was just as puzzling as that of his two comrades.

"Belnikov's been murdered," I told him. "Shot in his room."

Nikki gasped, but Boris's reaction was the one that interested me. He looked as if he'd been punched in the throat, and then he actually started to cry!

"Boris—" Nikki began, but he brushed past us, entering the elevator alone.

I turned to Nikki and saw that she appeared stunned.

"Nikki, I'm sorry. I didn't mean to blurt it out that way," I apologized.

"That's all right, Nick. Tell me what happened?"

I explained what had happened, and how Belnikov was found.

"The same way poor Martin Leonard was killed. Was it the same person?" she asked.

"It would appear so," I told her, not elaborating that it might have deliberately been meant to look that way.

"Nikki, I know you're shocked, but I'd like to ask you a few questions. Let's take this elevator," I suggested, as one of the others came down. We stepped in and started up.

"Did you talk to Belnikov about what we discussed?"

"What? No, I never had a chance. Now I never will."

I wondered if the information that made Belnikov so important was written down anywhere, or if it had died with him?

That possibility might justify my staying around a while longer, and helping Borga while I was at it.

When we reached the fifteenth floor Nikki rushed out ahead of me. When I caught up to her she was standing just outside the room and I could hear some commotion from within.

"What's going on?" I asked her.

"Boris," she said, pointing.

I looked inside and saw what she meant. Apparently, Boris had flipped, and he was in the process of cleaning up the room with Borga and his two men. The technicians were standing around gaping as the big man repeatedly resisted the three policemen's efforts to apprehend him.

Boris was like a mad bull and I had to stop him before Borga decided that the only solution was to shoot him. I looked around for something to use, then spotted one of the photographers. I grabbed his camera, with flash attachment, and rushed toward Boris.

I called out his name and he turned from the fallen inspector, who he was ready to stomp into the floor. Borga himself appeared to be going for his gun. He'd made up his mind that a possible international incident was better than getting stomped.

As Boris faced me, I pushed the camera close to his face and flipped the shutter. He suddenly became very concerned with trying to clear his eyes. Borga's two men were quick to take advantage, each grabbing a massive arm, while Borga applied the handcuffs to Boris's wrists.

Everyone in the room seemed to breathe a sigh of relief. Borga approached me, holding a handkerchief to a cut just over his left eyebrow.

"Mr. Crane, thank you. If for no other reason, you have just justified my decision to allow you to become involved in this investigation."

He turned to his men and said something short and, nursing their own wounds, they left the room with Boris, who had now become curiously docile.

"Where are they taking him?" the Russian woman demanded.

"They will detain him until he has calmed down enough to be questioned. I would like some explanation of his violent behavior," he told her. She clammed up and sat down next to Vladimir. "I have no choice but to assume that guilt, and possibly remorse, are the cause of his wild actions," Borga added.

"You think Boris is the killer?" I asked.

"I have not formed a definite opinion, but he will remain in custody until I do so."

That meant that Boris looked good for it, as far as Borga was concerned. It struck me, though, that if Boris had killed both Leonard and Belnikov, they would more than likely have died of broken necks.

THIRTY

In spite of the fact that Borga saw Boris as a prime suspect, he still went through the motions. Again, he allowed me to sit in on all of the interviews. Before we started, however, I suggested that he have the hotel doctor treat the wound on his head. He agreed, and once he was patched up with a small bandage he had a couple of uniformed men escort each person in.

For some unknown reason, he kept the major and Vladimir in the room while questioning the others. Maybe he just wanted to keep them where he could see them.

The whole process was very boring, because I felt there was nothing to be learned from the other competitors. My own thoughts were that the killer was going to turn out to be someone closely connected with Belnikov, perhaps even one of his own people. They might have found out about his intention to defect and had killed him rather than allow it to happen. That meant that their reactions to his death were all put on— or, at least, one of them was. Boris struck me as the type who wouldn't have done it unless he was directed to. The other two seemed perfectly capable of making such a decision on their own, and carrying it out as well.

It was quite late when the questioning was completed, and as we rose and stretched, Borga asked me, "Would you like to come along to headquarters and listen while I question the other man?"

I considered saying no, because I wanted to contact Hawk, but then decided to go along and see what Boris had to say.

We rode down in the elevator together, after he had given the major and Vladimir instructions not to attempt to leave the hotel. I had the feeling that he would have liked to take them in also, but he couldn't because of their airtight alibi—me.

I waved at Angel, who appeared to be going off duty, as we walked out of the hotel and then got into the inspector's car. We drove through the small village to a brick-and-stone building that was Borga's police headquarters. I followed him to the second floor where he maintained a cramped office.

He sat behind his desk heavily and rubbed dry hands over his face. I took a seat in a corner and crossed my legs, waiting for him to speak.

"Russians," he finally said, shaking his head. I got the distinct impression he didn't like them, and had to wonder if he wasn't allowing that dislike to cloud his judgment. Maybe he wanted one of them to be the killer.

"We have a dead American and a dead Russian," he continued, touching the bandage on his head. "Does it seem likely that they would be killed by the same person?"

"Yes," I said, and he looked at me in surprise. "If the motive for the murder had nothing to do with nationalities."

He stared at me a moment, then nodded his head. "Perhaps the matter of nationalities is clouding my view of the case, yes," he finally admitted.

"You have no particular love for the Russians?" I asked.

"My parents were killed by the Russians, during the war," he told me. "They had the misfortune to be in the wrong place at the wrong time. No, I have no particular love for the Russians. In fact," he went on, apologetically, "if you will forgive me for saying so, I do not have any particular liking for foreigners, in general."

"I understand," I told him.

"I am having the big Russian brought to the interrogation room," he told me. "No rubber hoses, I'm afraid," he added.

"I thought you told me you never watched American TV?"

He smiled. "Touché. Perhaps I have seen one or two of your American—what do you call them—cop shows?"

"Among other things, yes."

A uniformed man stuck his upper torso in the door to inform the inspector of something, probably the fact that Boris was ready to be questioned.

I followed Borga across the hall to another room, even smaller than his office; it looked like an old broom closet. In the room, Boris was seated on a three-legged stool so he wouldn't get too comfortable. He had an array of bruises on his face that I didn't believe had come from the scuffle in the hotel room. More than likely he had "fallen down" a lot on the way to police headquarters, while handcuffed. Borga cast a glance my way to see if I would react to the big man's appearance, and was apparently satisfied with what he saw.

"Does he speak English?" Borga asked me.

Remembering the two times he had spoken to me, I replied that he did, although I didn't know to what extent.

Borga began throwing questions at Boris, who appeared confused by the whole turn of events. Either he didn't understand what Borga was saying or didn't want to. He shook his head a couple of times, as if trying to clear it, but on the whole the entire interview was useless.

Borga, thoroughly disgusted, said something to one of the police officers, and then led me back to his office. He sat behind his desk and reached into a drawer, producing a bottle of scotch and two glasses. He held the bottle up to me and I nodded. He filled both glasses about a third of the way up, and then passed me one.

"What does his reticence indicate to you?" he asked.

"I think he's just confused."

"You believe he is innocent?"

"I do."

"Why?"

"First of all, he isn't smart enough to make a decision like that on his own."

"He could have been directed," Borga suggested.

"That's true, but I believe that the other two Russians are perfectly capable of doing their own killing."

He nodded and said, "What else?"

"If he had killed Leonard and Belnikov, I believe it would have been with his bare hands. Neither one of the bodies seemed bruised, or indicated in any way that they may have been in a fight before being shot. Unless your autopsy turned something up?"

He shook his head. "Your assumption is correct. Neither man was beaten first."

"Boris would use his hands, especially if he was in a rage—as he was with you and your men."

"You believe he was not acting?"

"I saw his eyes," I told him. "The man was crazy with rage—or grief. What set him off?"

"He entered the room abruptly and demanded to know where Belnikov was. One of the other Russians told him and when he started for the bathroom, one of my men blocked his way. He picked him up as if he were a toy and threw him across the room. My man is six-foot-one and weighs over two-hundred pounds, Mr. Crane. I must admit, it was very disconcerting."

"To say the least."

"At that point, I and my other man attempted to detain him, and a scuffle ensued," he told me, touching his bandage again.

"Scuffle is a pretty mild word for it," I told him.

"I agree."

"None of your lab men seemed very anxious to help," I remarked.

He shrugged that off. "They get paid to take pictures and sprinkle dust," he explained.

"What do you plan to do with Boris?" I asked.

"At the very least he assaulted three police officers," he explained. "I will hold him for a while."

"If he's lucky, there'll be another murder while he's locked up," I said.

"Please," he said, looking pained.

I raised my hand and said, "Sorry. It was just a comment."

"An ill-advised one, at best."

"Granted. Can I get a ride back?"

"Certainly," He shouted out the door, and then told me, "A car will be waiting downstairs. Thank you for your cooperation, Mr. Crane." He touched the bandage and added ruefully, "You've been very helpful, tonight."

THIRTY-ONE

When the patrol car dropped me off at the hotel I was ready for a hot bath and some sack time. Neither was to happen as soon as I had hoped. My carelessness was probably due to being overtired—or perhaps I instinctively knew that there was really no immediate danger. In any case, I used my key to enter my room, turned on the light and there he was, sitting on the couch with a gun pointed at me, perfectly capable of blowing me away with ease. It was Vladimir.

The hand with the gun was rock steady and this Vladimir bore no resemblance to the devastated Russian Borga and I had left in his apartment hours ago.

"Take a seat, please, Mr. Carter," he advised me, using my real name. I wondered if he had found something in my room that gave me away, or had he recognized me right from the beginning.

"Carter," I repeated, seating myself on the smaller chair next to the couch.

"Yes. You see, we know who you really are, and why you are here," he explained.

"We?"

"All of us. The major, Boris and I."

"And how do you know that?"

"Alexi told us. He told us that he was defecting, and

that an American agent would be meeting him here to get him to the United States."

"He told you all that?" I asked. I hadn't thought Belnikov would be confiding in anyone, least of all the people the Soviets had sent along to keep an eye on him.

They killed him.

Vladimir did something unexpected then: He put his gun away.

"I have not disarmed you, Mr. Carter, and I have put my own weapon away. That should tell you something."

"It tells me I'm confused," I admitted.

"Then I should explain. Boris did not kill Alexi, Mr. Carter."

"I agree."

"I am very happy to hear you say that. Truthfully, none of us killed him, and we would like you to find out who did."

"Why me? Why not do it yourselves?"

"We are not detectives, and we are not Nick Carter. Your reputation precedes you, and we cannot pretend that we are in your class."

"I'm flattered." That was not the kind of admission I was used to hearing from enemy agents, especially the Soviets.

"And just a little skeptical, I imagine," Vladimir added.

"To say the least."

"I cannot say that I blame you, but I can only ask that you believe that none of us are responsible for—Alexi's death," he said, sounding sincere.

"So, the Soviet Union wants me to find out who murdered their chess champ?" I asked, just to see how he'd handle it.

He handled it well. He shook his head and said, "Not the Soviet Union, Mr. Carter, not the Kremlin. Just the three of us."

"To keep yourselves out of trouble for letting him get killed?"

He shook his head slowly, staring at me.

"Listen, what did you think about his defecting?"

"We accepted it. It was what he wanted."

"And what are you going to tell them when you go back?"

He waited a moment before answering, then dropped it on me. "We are not going back, Mr. Carter."

"You're not. Well, then, where are you going?"

"We are going to the United States, with you."

"What?"

"We are defecting."

I was stunned for a moment, then asked, "All of you?"

"Yes."

"Was this a snap decision, brought on by Belnikov's death?"

"No. We intended to go along with him all along," he answered, rising and heading for the door. "I have the information that he was going to give to your country, Mr. Carter. Find out who killed him, and I'll give it to you."

"Wait a minute, wait a minute," I told him while he was opening the door to leave. "What's this all about?"

"I don't understand."

"Why are you doing this? Why is it so important that I find out who killed Belnikov? What was he to you?"

He looked down at the floor, then came to a decision and looked at me again. "My name is Vladimir Belnikov," he told me, and he left.

THIRTY-TWO

His family.

Vladimir and Boris, his sons?

The major, his wife? Sister?

It didn't really matter who was what. Apparently, if I was to believe Vladimir, they were his family, and he was taking them with him when he defected.

Again, if I was to believe Vladimir Belnikov's information did not die with him. And, if that was true, then it was worth it for me to stick around and continue to offer Inspector Borga my expertise in the murder investigation.

I called Nikki's room and she was in. "I'm coming over," I told her.

"Please, Nick, not tonight—"

"We have to talk, Nikki. I'm on my way."

I hung up on any further protests.

She let me in, wearing a thick, red robe that she kept wrapped tightly around her.

"What do you want, Nick?" she asked, sitting on the couch, her shoulders slumped.

"I want to know what was going on with you and Belnikov, Nikki. I don't think I buy the May-December bit."

"Well, I'm sorry if you don't buy it, but that's all I have to sell."

I tried another tactic. "You remember that I told you Belnikov planned to defect?"

She stared at me, then said, "He wouldn't talk about it . . . when I asked him . . . after I talked to you. He wouldn't admit it, but I figured you were right. Is that what got him killed?"

"Maybe. Did you know that he had a family?"

She shook her head. "He never mentioned one."

"What about the happy threesome?"

She frowned, not understanding.

"Vladimir, Boris and the major. How did he feel about them?" I asked, making it clearer.

She shrugged. "He said . . . he said they were his . . . family," she told me, then realized what she had said. "I thought he was just being sarcastic," she told me, frowning. "You mean those three, they're *really* his family?"

"It would appear so."

"That . . . that woman?"

I shrugged. "Wife, sister, I don't really know."

"And you?"

"I'm an expediter. I was going to expedite his trip to the United States, only I didn't know that he intended to take the whole crew with him."

"His family," she said again, as if she couldn't believe it.

"Look, Nikki, let's put that aside for now. When you left Belnikov to go down and play your match, how was he?"

"How was he? He was fine, he was alive."

"What was he doing?"

"He was working on chess problems, with that red-and-white piece chess set he had."

I thought back to the scene as I had found it after breaking the door in. The vase on the floor . . . a chess set, with the pieces set up for a problem? I remembered it, but there was something about it . . .

"It couldn't have been more than half-an-hour from

the time you came down until the time I went up. During those thirty minutes somebody got into that room, killed him, stuffed him in the tub and then got out again."

Belnikov must have struggled for that vase to have gotten knocked over. If that were the case, though, how did the killer shoot him, stuff him into the tub and then get out of the room in the short time it took Vladimir and myself to break down that door? And why had some of the blood in the tub dried in only a few minutes?

"Who do you think it was? One of . . . them?"

"I might have thought that, until I found out that they were his family," I told her. "Now I'm not so sure. In any case, Vladimir or the major couldn't have done it, because they were at the door, arguing with me. And Boris was downstairs with you, wasn't he?"

"I guess so."

"What do you mean you guess so?" I asked.

"Well, I was concentrating on my game, Nick, I wasn't keeping track of Boris."

"You mean he could have slipped out . . . no, he was still down there when I left. How could he get into the room and out without being seen?"

She shrugged. "I have no idea. Nick, I'm tired, I want to go to sleep."

So did I. I left and went back to my room. There was nobody with a gun waiting for me this time. I took that bath, and then went to bed.

THIRTY-THREE

I dreamed that night about red-and-white chess pieces, and woke up with that nagging, back-of-the-mind thought that there was something I'd missed. I got up, showered and decided not to order breakfast in my room. I'd stop downstairs for something a little later on. The first thing I wanted to do was go up to Belnikov's room and look around. They hadn't moved Vladimir and the major out of the room, mainly because the hotel was full and there was nowhere else to put them.

My knock was answered by the tiny major, who seemed none too glad to see me, but Vladimir stepped around her and asked me in. The major disappeared into her bedroom and left the two of us alone.

"She doesn't approve of me," I remarked.

"No. She was the only one of us who argued with Alexi vehemently against defecting, but he had made up his mind. Have you found out something that brings you here so early in the day?"

"I want to look around," I told him. I still referred to him by his last name, and he referred to the deceased by his first. I did not ask for clarification as to the relationship to one another. It wasn't that important.

"For what?"

I shrugged, saying, "I'll know when I see it. There's

just something eating at me, something that I saw, but didn't immediately comprehend."

"Very well," he agreed, and led the way into the room. It was unchanged. The pieces of vase had not been cleaned, although they had been dusted for prints. The only change was in the damp patch on the rug. It had since dried. On the dresser from which the vase had fallen was an empty ice bucket and a two-thirds empty bottle of vodka.

I made a slow circuit of the room, and finally stopped when I came to the chess set.

"Did he take this with him wherever he went?" I asked.

"Always."

I examined the position of the pieces, seeing if it resembled anything I had learned from Evan Clarke.

"Why the red-and-white instead of the traditional black-and-white?" I asked, touching a red rook. The pieces were made from hand-carved wood.

"Obvious reasons," he answered.

Black-and-white always struck me as reflecting evil and good. I wondered if the same could be said for red-and-white.

The position of the pieces didn't ring any bells with me, and I was about to walk away when something struck me as being wrong. Had the pieces been set up for the beginning of a game, it would have been obvious what the problem was, but spread out over the board like that, it had taken a few moments to sink in.

"Where's the red queen?" I asked Vladimir.

He looked at the board a moment, then said, "Perhaps it has been captured from the board?"

We took a moment to see what pieces had been swept away and the queen was not among them.

"It's gone," I told him, sure of it.

"The floor?" he said, bending down to look.

"No, I'm sure it's gone, Vladimir."

"Well, perhaps he lost it. What is the difference?"

"I don't know," I said, touching my chin. "I don't know for sure. It's the only thing in this room that sticks out," I added, "that really strikes me as wrong." That and the previously wet patch in the rug where the vase had fallen. I turned and looked at the pieces again, and at the artificial flowers that were strewn about. Why would a vase of artificial flowers have water in it?

"I do not see why this concerns you so," Vladimir complained. "You should be trying to find out—"

I put my hand on his arm, interrupting. "I am trying, Vladimir, I assure you. I'm just covering all bases."

"I don't understand that," he whined. "I assume it's some kind of American expression."

"It means I'm considering all possibilities," I clarified.

"Very well. Are you finished in here?" he asked.

"Yes, I'm finished."

"Please, let us go into the other room."

I followed him out and he seemed to calm down once we were out of that room.

"What is going to happen to Boris?"

"Well, he did assault three law officials," I told him. "They don't take kindly to that in this country."

"What will they do?"

I decided to try and set his mind at ease. "I think they'll just detain him for a short while. Perhaps even until the murderer—or murderers—of Martin Leonard and Alexi Belnikov are caught."

"That is unfair," he declared. I thought it an odd word for someone from the Soviet Union to use.

"Not if you think about it, Vladimir. Boris has a vicious temper. He's safer right where he is."

He considered that, then gave a short nod, as if it made sense to him.

"I have to go. I'll get back to you if I come up with anything," I promised.

"Very well."

I left and went downstairs to have some breakfast and mull over the meaning of the missing queen—if there was one. And also the damp patch in the rug. Small items, but they might turn out to be much larger in the scheme of things.

I stopped at the desk to say good morning to Angel, who didn't have any positive news about her search for the proper overseas operator.

"Unless whoever it was has forgotten about it," she added.

"I guess that's a possibility," I admitted.

"Having breakfast?" she asked. I nodded, afraid that she was going to ask to join me, in which case I'd have to turn her down. I was wrong, however, as she demonstrated when she said, "Well, I'm stuck back here for a while, so enjoy it."

"I'll try," I promised.

I went into the restaurant and ordered coffee, drank it slowly while I went over everything in my mind. Maybe I was making too much of the missing chess piece, but I didn't think a master like Belnikov would just lose a piece from a set that he carried everywhere with him, one that he'd probably had made up special for him.

I called the waiter over and ordered some breakfast, then asked him to bring a phone to the table.

I also thought that Borga was too good a cop not to have noticed that the piece was missing, and I decided to ask him about it.

THIRTY-FOUR

"In his hand?" I snapped into the phone. "Why the hell didn't you tell me that before?"

When he answered, Borga actually sounded sheepish about it. "I just thought to keep some things to myself," he said.

"You lied to me."

"About what?"

"You do watch a lot of American television, don't you?"

He laughed and pleaded guilty. I think it was the first time I'd heard him laugh.

"Okay, forget it," I told him. "Let me get it straight. He had the chess piece clenched in his right hand?"

"That's right."

"Well, that couldn't have happened after he'd been shot, not shot in the head like that. He had to have died instantly. He must have had the piece in his hand when he was shot."

"Perhaps he was simply making a move when it happened, and his hand closed on it convulsively."

"I guess that's a possibility," I agreed, but he didn't believe it, or else he would have mentioned it to me in the beginning.

"Is there anything else that you're holding back from

me, Inspector?" I asked formally.

"No, Mr. Crane, nothing that I can think of at the moment," he told me.

"Well, if you do happen to have an attack of the guilts about something else you're not letting me in on, will you give me a call?"

"Attack of the guilts," he repeated. "I quite like that phrase. Yes, indeed, if I have an attack of the guilts, I will call you immediately."

"Thanks."

When I hung up the waiter replaced the phone with my breakfast. I hadn't realized how hungry I was until the food was placed in front of me, so I went to work on two things at once: my stomach, and the murders.

They were connected, of that I was sure. Maybe not committed by the same person, but connected nevertheless. Martin Leonard had been blown away for some unknown reason, but Belnikov's murder had to be to keep him from defecting with whatever valuable information it was that he had. Only now, even though he was dead, it appeared that the information was not lost to us. All I had to do was find out who killed Belnikov, and then get his family to the United States, and the information would be ours.

A piece of cake, right?

That chess piece in Belnikov's hand bothered me. He might have simply had it in his hand when he was shot, but then again, when he became aware of what was going to happen, he may have grabbed it in an attempt to leave a clue to the identity of his killer.

So what we had here were all of the classic ingredients of the perfect mystery story: a locked room, a dying message and a hotel full of suspects.

Just what I didn't need.

After breakfast I decided to go back upstairs and talk to Vladimir again. If he was so close to Belnikov, then he had to know something that would help me. There must have been something Belnikov had said or done. All I had to do was take Vladimir through the past few days, step-by-step.

I waved at Angel as I passed the desk and took the elevator to the fifteenth floor. I knocked on the door, but got no answer. With what had already happened inside that suite, I decided not to just walk away and accept that. I knocked on the door again, then pounded. Even if Vladimir had gone out, I didn't think the woman had. Something was wrong, and I wasn't going to find out what it was standing out in the hall.

I took out my kit and unlocked the door. I went in low, with Wilhelmina out in front of me. If I was wrong, I'd apologize.

I wasn't wrong.

The major was lying in the doorway to her bedroom, her head a bloody mess. She was on her face, as if she'd been shot while running out of her room. I knew that each bedroom in this suite had its own bath, and I knew what I'd find in hers.

I stepped over her and into the room beyond. From appearances, nothing was amiss, but I only had to turn around to dispel that fantasy.

Vladimir was in the bathtub—just as Leonard and Belnikov had been.

I called Borga.

"Do you have something for me, Mr. Crane?"

"Yes, I do," I told him. "I've got two more."

THIRTY-FIVE

Borga's expression was even grimmer than usual when he came in and saw the dead woman.

"She was coming out of the room when she was shot," he observed.

"I agree. Either walking or running."

"Considering what is in the bathtub," he remarked, "I would say she was most probably running."

He stepped over her, and I followed him into the bathroom. He stood there looking at the body in the tub and the lines in his face seemed to deepen. "One shot in the head," he said bending over as if to examine the body.

"I've already checked his hands," I told him. He gave me a sharp look and I added, "I didn't want anymore surprises, and I thought I'd save you the temptation to keep something else from me."

He checked anyway, then stood up and asked, "How do I know you are not keeping something from me?"

I raised my right hand and said, "Word of honor."

Borga's crew followed into the room, and he and I left to make room for them.

"This was very recent," I told him, explaining that I had spoken to them both that morning.

"So the time period was only as long as it took you to

have breakfast," he said.

"That's it."

We stepped back over the major's body, and I was struck by the thought that I'd never heard her called anything but "the major."

In the other room I commented, "At least this does one positive thing for us."

"What is that?"

"It clears Boris Belnikov."

"It clears—I beg your pardon? Did you say Belnikov? Isn't that—"

"Have a seat and I'll explain," I told him. He sat on the couch and I told him about Vladimir coming to me the night before and asking me to find the killer of his father. Even though I still wasn't sure of the relationship, I padded it a bit to make up for not mentioning Belnikov's defection.

"I see we both held something out on each other," he remarked when I was finished.

"Well, not really, Inspector. I only got the information last night."

"And we spoke on the phone earlier this morning, at which time you failed to mention it to me."

"I wanted to talk to Vladimir once again, just to make sure I bought his story. That's when I came up here and found them."

"How did you get in?" he asked.

"Under the circumstances, Inspector, couldn't we overlook that?" I asked.

"Yes, I suppose we could."

I sat down next to him and tried to think while there was bedlam going on around us. "I don't feel it's necessary to go through all the interviews again," I commented. "We're bound to get the same answers."

"I agree," he sighed, and I wondered if he had slept at all since we met.

"What do you suggest?" he asked.

"I think that's fairly easy," I told him. "Let's talk to Boris."

"That would seem a logical next step," he agreed.

He left one of his men in charge of the crime scene, and we went down to his car to drive to his office.

In the car I asked, "By the way, was Belnikov killed by the same gun that killed Leonard?"

"Yes, and so, I suspect, were those two upstairs. I believe the killer is the same person."

"Or at least, the same gun."

"Yes."

"This lets Boris off the hook."

"Not as far as the charges of assaulting police officials," he pointed out.

"Well, maybe we could use that to get him to come clean."

We rode the rest of the way in silence, each of us occupied by our own thoughts. I was wondering if Boris knew anything that could help us, and if he did, I wondered if he'd tell us.

We waited in Borga's office while they moved Boris to the small interrogation room. We lowered the level on his office bottle while we waited.

"What was the big Russian's relationship to the older man?" he asked me.

I shrugged. "Either son or nephew, I guess."

"And the woman?"

"Not sure about that, either. Wife, sister . . . lover?"

He made a face and drained his glass, showing what he thought of her in any context. Finally, one of his men stuck his head in the door and said something.

"Boris is ready," Borga said. He put the bottle away and led the way.

Boris was once again seated on a stool, looking like a big, shaggy bear seated on a tree stump. He hadn't shaven, which only enhanced his shaggy look.

I didn't know what Borga had in mind, but as we entered the room I leaned over and suggested, "Let's try English, first."

He nodded and motioned for me to do the honors.

"Boris, I have some bad news for you," I told the big man. Aside from a movement of his eyebrows, and a slight shifting of his wide shoulders, he didn't seem to react, or understand.

"Vladimir and the major are dead," I said in a monotone voice. "Just like Alexi, just like the American. They're all gone, Boris, all but you."

Borga was about to speak, but I put my hand on his arm to stop him. I wanted to give it time to sink in. When it finally did, the tears came. Borga and I stood there and watched the big man cry. It was an odd feeling. His mouth moved, but no sound came out, just rivers of tears streaming from his eyes. Finally, he regained control of himself and the tears stopped. He sat on the stool, shoulders slumped forward, hands hanging to the floor, shaking his head.

There was a rumbling in the room, and then we realized that it was Boris speaking.

"I beg your pardon?" Borga asked.

Boris cleared his throat and repeated what he had said. "They sent someone."

"Who?" Borga asked.

"The Kremlin."

"Who did they send?" I asked.

He shrugged. "I do not know. They sent someone to watch us, to watch Alexi."

"Why?" Borga asked.

"They knew . . . they knew he was considering defection. They let us come with him, to watch him, but Vladimir knew that we would be watched also. Vladimir said that once he had made contact with you," Boris went on, "they would probably try to kill him. That was why we all stayed in the same room." He shrugged his shoulders and added, "It did not matter."

Borga was looking at me strangely, and I knew the wheels were turning.

Boris looked at Borga and asked, "I can see my mother and my brother?"

"You will see them soon enough," he told the big Russian. He spoke shortly to one of his men, then turned angry eyes on me and said, "Let's go back to my office. I would like to talk to you."

THIRTY-SIX

"Close the door," Borga told me. He went around behind his desk, took out the bottle, poured himself a drink and then put the bottle away.

I was in trouble.

"I would like to hear the entire story, Mr. Crane," he told me, "if that is your real name."

"It's as good as any," I told him. "Don't I get a drink?"

He pointedly sipped his drink and set his glass down on his desk top. "What are you, the CIA?" he asked. "Some other branch of American Intelligence?"

"Inspector—"

He pointed a finger at me and said, "I would advise you to tell me the truth, or something pretty near to it, Mr. Crane, or you won't be leaving this building tonight. In fact, I might even allow you to share a room with the Russian. Now, as they say on your American TV, 'what is the story'?"

"The story," I began, making it look like I had decided to tell all, "is just what Boris told you. Belnikov was defecting, I was sent in to get him out. Now, it looks as though the Russians sent somebody in to keep me from doing that."

"Whoever it was did a very good job," he pointed out.

"That's true. You mind if I have that drink now?"

He thought about it a moment, then took the bottle out, poured some into my glass, seemed about to put the bottle away, then thought better of it and left it on the desk. I picked up the glass and took a sip.

"Belnikov is dead. Why are you still here?" he asked.

"His information, it didn't die with him. Vladimir came to me and told me that he would give me the information if I found out who killed the old man."

"You believed him?"

"Well, at first I thought that maybe he was just trying to cover up the fact that he killed him, but he finally convinced me."

"You believed him about the information?"

"It didn't really matter whether I believed him or not. As long as there was a chance he was telling the truth, I had to go along."

He considered that for a few moments, then asked, "And the big Russian? You believe he might have the information, also?"

"If he does, he's the last chance I have of getting it. Would you let me talk to him alone?"

He set his jaw, looking stubborn.

"Look, Inspector, the only problem you have is that I didn't level with you—tell you the truth—from the beginning. You have to understand, I didn't really have a choice in the matter. Nothing's really changed. I'd still like to see the killer or killers get caught. What do you say?"

Once again he took a few moments to sort out his thoughts, then finished his drink and put away the bottle. He got up, opened the door and shouted something to one of the men outside. Then he sat back down and pointed his finger at me.

"I want to know everything he says to you, Mr. Crane."

"Are you going to bug the room?"

"I will take your word for it."

"Why so trustful?"

"Because this time, if I find out that you lied to me, or kept something from me, you will have a very difficult time getting out of Switzerland, I promise you. Understood?"

"Understood."

When Boris was ready they put me in the interrogation room with him, alone. Borga had said he wouldn't bug the room, but I figured that was because the room was already bugged.

"Boris," I began, "do you want to get out of here?"

He didn't react. He probably didn't care whether he ever got out or not.

"Boris, Alexi was your father, wasn't he?"

He looked at me and said, "Yes."

"You know why he was killed, don't you?"

"To keep him from defecting."

"I think, more importantly, it was to keep my people from getting the information that he promised to bring with him."

I waited to see if that would sink in, then asked, "Would you agree with that?"

"Yes," he said, after a pause to think about it.

"Boris, do you know what that information was?"

He looked confused, and that kept him silent. He had nobody to tell him what to think, and he wasn't equipped to handle it by himself.

"Boris, you don't want the deaths of your family to be for nothing, do you? I don't think you do."

"No."

"You know the information, don't you?"

He didn't answer.

"Boris, I think you do, and I think Alexi and Vladimir —as well as your mother—would want you to see that, even if they didn't make it, the information did. You and the information. I can get you both out, but you've got to be able to give me the information. Can you?"

"Yes," he finally admitted.

"Do you want me to get you out? Out of here, and out of the country?"

"Yes, but—"

"But what?" I asked. He was frowning, because he was thinking, and he wasn't used to that. I had a feeling I knew what he was going to say.

"I want to know who killed my family."

"You do know," I tried to tell him. "Your country sent another agent, to see that—"

"No, I want to know who the person is," he told me. Suddenly, he set his big jaw and looked me in the eye. "I won't give you any information until you find out who killed them."

A fine time for him to start thinking for himself, I thought.

Then he went even further.

"I will stay here," he said, pointing to the floor, "until you find the killer."

That much made sense. If he was here, then he wouldn't end up dead, too.

"Okay, Boris," I told him, standing up. "You've got a deal." He frowned at me, and I said, "I agree to your terms."

He nodded shortly, then resumed staring at the floor. I knocked on the door and was allowed out.

In Borga's office, I relayed the conversation, even though I was certain he had heard it all. When I was done, he was satisfied that I had told him everything.

"Very well," he said, "we are back where we started. We must find the killer, though our reasons for it differ."

"Inspector, have you told me everything?" I asked.

"I have given you all of the information I have," he said. However, I sensed a "but" on the end of that sentence, and pushed him a little. "There's nothing that you feel is insignificant that you've left out?"

"Only—" he began, then stopped, seeming to reconsider.

"Only what?"

He made a face and said, "It is just the way Belnikov was holding that chess piece in his hand. Rather odd . . ."

"In what way?" I asked, feeling like I was pulling teeth.

"Well, it was more out of his hand than it was in," he explained, holding a pencil up to illustrate. "The head of the piece was in his hand, and the rest was hanging out. In fact, his little finger was looped around the face of the piece," he added, looping his finger around the eraser on the end of the pencil.

"Where is the piece?" I asked.

"Downstairs. Would you like to see it?"

"I would."

I didn't know what seeing it would tell me, but it didn't hurt to look. He picked up the phone and spoke to someone, and we waited for the piece to arrive. In a few minutes a man entered, carrying a plastic bag containing the red queen. The man handed it to Borga, who extended it to me.

"Show me how Belnikov was holding it," I told him.

He removed the piece from the bag, then held it in his right hand so that his little finger was covering the queen's face, but the rest of the body was sticking out. All the while, I had envisioned Belnikov holding the piece clutched in his palm. This was a new development, but what did it mean, if anything?

He stared at the piece in his hand, puzzled. "Do you think it was deliberate?" he asked.

"I don't know," I said, standing up. "The man was brilliant," I reasoned, "he had a quick mind. If he knew he was going to be killed, and he didn't panic, then he may have meant it as a message."

I started for the door, while Borga sat at his desk, still staring at the piece hanging from his hand.

"Mr. Crane," he called quietly.

I turned. "Yes?"

"Who are you working for?" he asked.

"Well, right now," I suggested, "let's just say I'm working for you."

THIRTY-SEVEN

When Borga's man dropped me at the hotel I had it in my mind to go up to my room and contact Hawk, something I had put off long enough. I was intercepted, however, by Angel, who was apparently off duty.

"Nick. Got time for a drink?" she asked, coming around the desk to stand in front of me. If anything, she looked younger and prettier than she had since I'd met her, and I really had been using her rather mercilessly.

"I guess I could use a drink. Sure, why not?"

We went into the bar, grabbed a booth, and ordered our drinks.

"Just get back from police headquarters?" she asked.

"Uh, yeah, I was helping Inspector Borga as much as I could. I have been all along."

"Is that why you haven't been able to tell me anything? Because you've been working with the police?"

"Yes, I'm sorry—"

"Liar," she said calmly, just as the waiter arrived with our drinks.

When he left I said, "What did you call me?"

"A liar. C'mon, Nick, level with me," she said, leaning forward.

"What are you, CIA or something?"

She was the second person to ask me that in the past hour.

"I swear to you, Angel, I'm not CIA." I told her.

"That's just the kind of answer I expected you to give me. It tells me what you're not, but not what you are."

"What makes you think I'm anything?"

"People are dying around here, Nick, and you're right in the middle of it."

I tweaked her nose and told her, "You're too nosy for your own good."

"I know you really mean that, but I can't help it. At least tell me if there's something I can do to help."

I shook my head and said, "I'm afraid not, Angel. That is, unless you've located that overseas operator?"

"I'm sorry, Nick, but I haven't."

"Oh, well," I said, and finished my drink. "I've got to get upstairs, Angel."

"Do you have a match today?" she asked.

I'd forgotten all about the tournament. I wondered when Nikki's next contest was. I wanted to talk to her again about Belnikov and the other Russians.

"I do, yes. I'll have to check the board to see who my opponent is."

"You see?" she said. "If all you were here for was chess, you'd already know who you were playing. I'll bet you forgot all about the tournament, didn't you?"

"I'll see you later," I told her. Dropping some money on the table for the drinks, I headed for my room to contact Hawk. I hoped he had something to tell me that would fit with everything I already knew and hand me a killer.

"I've been worried, N3," he said when I had the television focused in on him.

"I appreciate that, sir," I told him.

"I was afraid I was going to have to put another man on this assignment, and we are a bit tight on personnel, right now."

He was serious.

"There have been a few developments, sir," I told him.

He frowned. "Disturbing ones?"

"That's the kind," I confirmed, nodding.

"I see. Well, let's hear them."

I gave it all to him, the two additional murders, the deal I'd made, first with Vladimir, then with Boris, and the fact that the local constabulary knew most of what was going on.

When I related that last bit to him he said, "I hope you were at least discreet with the local law."

"Yes sir, very. He doesn't know who I work for."

"We can be thankful for that, in any case. What about this Boris. Do you believe he really has Belnikov's information?"

"I don't think we have any choice but to play it as if he does, sir. It's the only chance we have of getting it."

"I agree. Very well, I will continue to hold a plane ready for your use. You will let me know when you need it."

"Very well, sir. Thank you."

"Be careful, N3. I don't have the men immediately at my disposal to bail you out should you be in need of assistance."

"I'll keep that in mind, sir. What was the additional information you had on Martin Leonard?"

"Only that, some years ago, he was fairly active in the American Nazi movement."

"We're dealing with the Soviets here, sir, not the Germans," I pointed out.

"I am quite aware of that, N3," he said, testily. "But it is something out of the ordinary that popped up in his file. I thought you should be aware of it."

"I understand, sir, and I appreciate it. Thank you."

I allowed his visage to fade away and then returned my equipment to my suitcase. After that I sat on the bed and tried to put all of the pieces together.

What did Martin Leonard's past affiliation with the American Nazi group have to do with all of this? Were the Germans also interested in Belnikov and his information? Was I dealing with German agents here as well as a Soviet agent? If that were the case, it only muddled matters further. Who killed Belnikov and his family, and who killed Martin Leonard—the Germans, the Russians? Or someone else?

What did the missing chess piece that showed up in Belnikov's hand have to do with anything? A dying message, or did he just happen to be holding it when he got shot? And what about the way he was holding it, with his little finger covering the queen's face?

And why the red Queen? Why not the white? Would he have grabbed it if it had been black?

Suddenly things started falling into place, but I didn't like where they were pointing. A red queen, meaning Soviet, and the fact that he had picked up the queen, out of all the available pieces, might have meant a Soviet woman. The only Soviet woman involved in the affair so far was the major, who had turned out to be Belnikov's wife. Did she kill him because of his flirtation with Nikki? And if so, who killed her, and Vladimir Belnikov? Could the two murders—first Belnikov's, then that of his son and wife—possibly be that unrelated? And all unrelated to that of Martin Leonard? How many murderers were we dealing with here?

The question was very unsettling.

THIRTY-EIGHT

My next step was to talk to Nikki again. I decided not to call her room first, because if for some reason she didn't want to talk to me, I didn't want to warn her that I was coming.

Nikki's complete turnaround was also puzzling to me. She didn't seem like the kind of woman who would be attracted to an older man, not even one as brilliant as Belnikov. What could she have been after? What was it she thought he could do for her? Advance her rating in the chess world? She was already considered by most to be the finest female player in the world. And why come on to me if all the while her target was Belnikov?

I walked down the hall to her room and knocked on the door. She answered almost immediately, wearing a terry cloth bathrobe. It was obvious she had nothing on underneath, and the ends of her hair were wet.

"I just got out of the shower," she told me.

"I'd like to come in and talk with you."

"I just got out of the shower, Nick," she repeated.

"You don't really have to be shy with me, Nikki, do you?" I asked her.

Her face underwent a couple of changes in expression as she decided how to play it. She surprised me with her decision. Her face broke into a wry smile and she told

181

me, "I guess not. Let me change."

I watched as she walked to the bedroom, and she very deliberately dropped her robe to the floor before she got to the door. I watched her undulating buttocks until she disappeared from view, and I wondered what was going through her mind now. With Belnikov gone had she now decided to turn her attention back to me?

I walked over to the coffee table where she had a chess set all ready for a game. Her set was black-and-white, and the pieces were cheap plastic, but it was generally the same size as Belnikov's carved wood, red-and-white set. I picked up the queen and held it in my hand, the way Inspector Borga had demonstrated in his office.

My little finger curled around the queen's head, completely cutting the face from view. If the little piece had eyes that could see, they would have been effectively blindfolded.

The queen would have been blind. Or, possibly, asleep.

I was still staring at the piece, that last word going through my mind, when I heard Nikki call from the next room.

I didn't know how many times she had called my name, because I had been so affected by my last thought that I knew I hadn't heard her the first time.

"Be there in a minute," I answered finally. I replaced the queen on the board and walked to the bedroom.

"Nikki?" I called as I entered.

"I'm here," she called out quietly. I turned my head and saw her standing by the doorway to the bathroom. She was naked, and she was holding those big breasts in her hands, her thumbs playfully brushing her distended nipples.

"We have a lot of lost time to make up for, Nick, darling," she said, approaching me. When she was close enough she put her arms around me and plastered herself to me. Her mouth was alive and hungry on mine. In seconds we were on the bed like two starving people at a feast, and when it was over we lay side-by-side, catching our breath.

"I guess I've been pretty silly," she told me.

"About what?"

"Belnikov, and the way I've treated you. I'm sorry, Nick," she apologized.

"That's all right, Nikki," I told her, assuring her that I understood.

We made love again soon after that, and then she said she had to get ready for her next match. I put all of the questions I had for her aside, letting her think that she effectively distracted me with the offer of her beautiful body.

I was distracted, but not totally. Staring at that plastic chess piece had made some pieces of the puzzle come together in my mind, and I believed I knew what Belnikov was trying to say by holding the red queen just the way he did. I needed some background checks—extensive background checks—before I could be sure I was right, before I could act on my theory, or reveal it to Borga for his thoughts.

I rose and got dressed, and Nikki pushed herself up against me again, giving me a kiss designed to keep me distracted for days to come.

"I'll see you after the match," she promised.

"I'll be waiting," I told her, and left.

THIRTY-NINE

I went back to my room and contacted Hawk again, who was surprised to hear from me so soon. I told him what I wanted, and gave him the names of the people I wanted the background checks on. I reiterated the fact that I wanted extensive background checks on each of the people, and that I hoped he would get back to me as soon as possible. He promised he would.

Next, I phoned Borga and told him what I wanted. I told him I wouldn't be able to tell him why until I had some more information, but that I would get back to him as soon as I could. Meanwhile, I suggested he have Boris ready to move as soon as he heard from me. He agreed to go along with me up to a certain point, after which he would want a complete explanation.

I went downstairs to watch Nikki's match, which she won. Afterward we had a victory drink in the bar and I put my plan into effect.

"Boris will be back in the hotel soon," I told her, "maybe as soon as tonight."

"Oh, really. In the same room?"

"I believe so. It's the only room that's empty."

"I guess they figure he's not the killer then, huh?"

"Oh, no, they're pretty sure he's not," I told her, not mentioning anything about the family relationship between all the Russians. "He was being held more on the assault charge then any suspicion of murder."

"I see. Are they dropping the assault charge?"

"I was able to persuade the detective in charge that he was simply overcome with grief. He was very close to Belnikov, but then I guess you know that."

"I do, indeed. Boris didn't like me at all. I think he was even jealous of the attention Alexi was paying me. He especially objected to being sent into town with me that day you saw us. I hope he doesn't come near me, Nick. I mean, maybe he'll think I had something to do with Alexi's death, or the death of his friends."

"Why would he think that?" I asked.

"I told you. He doesn't like me."

"Well, we'll try and make sure he doesn't come near you," I assured her.

She got up and asked me if I wanted to come to her room with her. I told her that perhaps we'd have dinner together, and then go to her room, but that I wanted to talk to the police about something. She said okay and left.

I went looking for Martine Dupree, and found her in the game room, watching her husband play.

"Hello, Martine," I greeted.

She looked at me gracing me with a smile and a nod.

"I hope there are no hard feelings, Martine," I told her.

She looked at me for a moment with those beautifully shaped eyes, then seemed to relent a little as she said, "No hard feeling, Nicholas."

"Good. Maybe you'll prove it to me by having a drink with me while your husband is, ah, occupied?"

She considered it a moment, stealing a look at her husband, then said, "Very well. Just to prove there are no hard feelings."

We went to the bar and sat at the same booth that Nikki and I had just vacated. The waiter, who had served not only Nikki and myself, but both Angel and me earlier, gave me a wise look as he took our orders.

"You have not been around so much," she scolded me.

"I've been assisting the police in their investigation of these murders," I explained.

"Ah, you are a policeman in your country?"

"I've had some experience with these matters," I told her.

"It's horrible, is it not. I do not feel safe in my own room," she told me.

"What about Andre?"

"Andre is a—how do you say—powder puff? He is no protection, I assure you. Ah, it must be those horrible Russians behind the whole matter," she confided.

"The Russians are the ones getting killed," I reminded her.

"And poor Martin," she lamented. "Poor, sweet, Martin."

"Did you know Martin well?" I asked.

"I . . . knew him at one time, yes," she said, very carefully.

"Well, I don't think you'll have to worry about the Russians anymore, since most of them are dead."

"And that large one, he is in the hands of the police, no?"

"He is now, but he'll be released, perhaps as soon as tonight," I told her.

"That is so?" she asked, wide-eyed.

"Oh, I don't think you have to worry, Martine. He'll probably be told to stay in his room. The same room, by the way, where they were all killed."

"I see," she said, slowly. She checked her watch and said, "I should get back. Andre should be just about ready to resign."

She rose and said, "Thank you for the drink, Nicholas. Perhaps we can meet again, later this evening?"

"Perhaps, Martine."

She smiled and left the restaurant/bar for the game room. I paid the waiter, who was still eyeing me with awe, and said, "I die in bed, my friend."

He smiled widely and nodded his head, indicating that this was the way he would like to go, too.

I didn't tell him that, in my business, that was the one way I didn't figure to go.

FORTY

Angel was next.

She was on the desk, and I stopped by to make some idle chit-chat, then let it slip about Boris being released.

"He's coming back here?" she asked in surprise.

"Yeah, same room, too."

"Are they crazy? Why don't they keep him locked up?" she asked.

I shrugged. "They don't figure him for the killer, and they're putting the assault down to grief. He's off the hook."

"Well, I hope he doesn't come near me," she said, shivering.

"Don't worry, I'll protect you," I said, putting my hand on her arm.

"I'll look forward to that," she said. As I was about to leave the desk area she said, "Oh, Nick, I almost forgot. You got a message."

"What is it?"

She frowned and said, "I hope it makes sense to you. The man just said to tell you that the birdman called."

Hawk. He'd gotten that information for me pretty quickly.

"Thanks, Angel, it makes sense."

"You are with the CIA, aren't you?" she asked.

I held up my right hand and said, "I swear I'm not. I used to be a boy scout, though."

"Cute."

"I was in my boy scout uniform," I told her, and went to the elevator.

Back in my room I established contact with Hawk, who had some information for me on one of the names I'd given him.

"We already had files on the players, so we just had to go a little deeper, N3. This lady's background was simple, because most of the early stuff appears to be fabricated."

"I thought it might. She was given a phony background as cover."

"How did you figure it out, N3?" he asked.

It was too complicated to explain to him at that moment, so I told him I would when I got back.

"Very well. I'll wait to hear from you."

I broke the connection.

I called Borga, and suggested that we move Boris back to his hotel room tonight.

"Why?"

"When you get here I'll tell you," I promised. "Let him come in alone, collect his key and go to his room, then come in and meet me in his room. I'll be in there already, waiting for him."

"The explanation had better be good, Mr. Crane."

"It will be," I told him, and hung up.

The hook was set, now all I had to do was attach the bait, and that would be accomplished with the arrival of Boris at the hotel.

Then all I had to do was sit and wait for the lady with the phony background to make a try at him. He was the last link to Belnikov's information. With him gone, her mission would be accomplished.

I was sure the murderer was a woman. That was Belnikov's message by holding the queen in his hand.

The next thing was the fact that the piece was red, indicating that the woman was a Soviet woman, or a Soviet agent. The final thing was the way he held the piece, with his little finger covering her face. That was to indicate that the woman was asleep—or a "sleeper" or "deep cover" agent, planted years ago for such time as it would become necessary to activate her.

The only thing I still had to find out was why she had killed Martin Leonard. I hoped to be able to ask her that once I caught her trying to kill Boris.

Assuming, of course, that I could keep Boris from killing her first.

FORTY-ONE

I waited in Boris' room that evening, and as it approached the time that Borga said he'd bring him by, I was hoping to God he wouldn't get shot in the elevator on his way up.

Suddenly the phone rang and I picked it up.

"Yeah."

"On his way up," Borga said, probably calling from the house phone.

"You watch him get in the elevator?" I asked.

"Yes."

"Okay."

I hung up and opened the front door so I could look out at the elevator. I watched as the numbers lit up, and then when it reached the fifteenth floor I watched the doors open and breathed a little easier when I saw Boris walk out.

He came to the door and I said, "Hello, Boris."

"Mr. Crane. The inspector said my coming here would help you find the killer of my family."

"It will, Boris, it will. Come on in." I ushered him into the room, checked the hall, then closed the door.

"How will this help?" he asked.

"Well, Boris, what I'm hoping is that whoever killed the others will try to kill you now. We will be able to prevent it, so you don't have to worry."

"It is the killer who should worry," he told me. "If he attempts to kill me, he will find it a difficult task to escape with his own life," he promised.

"The killer is a woman, Boris."

That didn't faze him. "A killer is a killer," he said, and it sounded like a pretty profound thing for him to say.

"I agree," I told him. "The inspector and one or two of his men will be up here soon enough. Why don't you get comfortable? You must be glad to be out of that cell."

He shrugged. "It doesn't matter," he said, sitting on the couch.

I wondered if Borga, his man and myself would be able to keep Boris from killing the killer when the time came. Next time, I wouldn't have a camera. There was a knock on the door and I let Borga in. He was alone.

"Where are your men?" I asked.

"One in the lobby, and one on the roof."

"Just the two of us here, huh?" I asked, looking pointedly at Boris.

"That's all we'll need," he assured me. Which meant that next time he wouldn't think so long before using his gun. He still had the bandage over his eye as a reminder of the last time.

"If you say so."

"Could I speak to you a moment?" he asked, walking away from the couch where Boris sat.

I followed him and he asked, "Will you tell me what you're up to now?"

"From the way you've deployed your men, I think you've pretty much guessed," I told him.

"You are going to use him as bait for the killer."

"That's right." I told him what I had figured out from the chess piece in Belnikov's hand, and what I had done to set Boris up as bait.

"You could be right," he agreed.

"And I could be wrong, but either way, we shoul

find out pretty soon. Did you bring what I asked?"

"I did." He was carrying a large attaché case, and now he put it on the coffee table and opened it. Inside was a bullet-proof vest. He lifted it out to show it to me.

"What is that?" Boris asked.

"It's a bullet-proof vest, Boris, for your protection," I told him.

"I do not need such a thing."

"You do unless you yourself are bullet proof," I said. He made a face and waved his hand.

"Boris, I believe someone is going to try to kill you, perhaps tonight. I also believe it will come as a simple knock on the door and a gunshot."

"You do not think the killer will follow her pattern?" Borga asked.

"I don't think she can afford to play around this time. It's going to be in and out, as fast as she can make it. She might know that it's a trap, but she's got to get Boris, or all the other killings will have been for nothing."

"Again, it would appear that you are making sense," Borga agreed.

"Now we have to make him see it our way," I said, indicating Boris.

Boris was adamant about not wearing the vest, but we finally got him to agree to put it on, underneath his shirt, before answering the door.

"I would like something to eat," he said, after the arguing was over.

"You'll have to call for it yourself, I'm afraid," I told him. "I don't want anyone to know that you're not alone."

He picked up the phone and struggled with room service—they trying to understand him, and he trying to understand them—until they finally had his order correct.

I spread the vest over the back of the couch, so it would be easily accessible to Boris.

"We might as well get comfortable," I told Borga,

removing my jacket. He raised his eyebrows as he saw Wilhelmina in the holster under my left arm, but said nothing.

"Don't you have a chess match?" he asked me.

I waved the thought away with my hand and said, "That's the least of my worries at this stage of the game."

Borga removed his jacket, also. He wore what looked to be a .38 caliber revolver in a hip holster of his left side.

Boris just sat on the couch, staring at the floor, every so often throwing a glance first at the room where his father was killed, then over at what was his mother's room.

"How about a drink?" I asked Borga.

"I admit I can use one," he replied.

I went looking for a bottle and remembered that there had been one in Belnikov's room. I was in there when I heard a knock on the door. I heard Borga yell, "No, wait," and, hurrying to get back into the front room, I pulled Wilhelmina from her holster. As I entered the front room again, I saw Borga behind Boris, trying to keep him from opening the door, but to no avail. The door was open and I heard one shot. Borga pulled his gun as Boris was thrown back from the door, apparently from the force of the first shot. I heard a second shot and heard Borga shout out in pain. I had to hurtle over Boris to reach the door, and by the time I did there was no one there.

"Damn!" I shouted. I looked back, torn between chasing the assailant and checking to see if Borga was all right. He solved that dilemma for me by shouting, "Go ahead, go ahead!"

I jumped out into the hall, crouching low in case of gunfire. When there was none I had to decide which direction the assailant might have gone, up or down. From the position of the elevator, I was sure he hadn't gone in there, so I ran to the stairway, hoping I'd be able to hear him and determine whether he—or, if my theory was right, she—was going up or down.

I broke through the exit door, once again going low, with my gun out in front of me. I stopped to listen for footsteps and heard none. I took this to mean that the assailant had gone up to the roof, because had the assailant gone down, I would still be able to hear footsteps. I didn't think he or she had entered at another floor, because the exit doors were locked from the staircase.

So, I made a decision and started up to the roof. If I was wrong, then maybe Borga's man downstairs would catch the shooter. If I was right, then Borga's other man and myself would have him or her trapped on the roof.

As I reached the door to the roof I heard an exchange of gunshots outside and knew I'd made the right decision. I went through the door and went into an immediate roll. I bumped into someone lying on the roof, and then realized that it was Borga's man. He was injured, but appeared to be alive.

It was dark on the roof with the only light of any kind coming from a half moon. I stayed where I was, flat down on the roof, listening.

"You can't get off this roof," I yelled out.

There was no reply, but I could hear someone scurrying about, probably looking for some other way off the roof. I didn't know for sure that there wasn't some other way off, but I was hoping to make the shooter think so.

I took the opportunity to feel for a pulse in the downed man's neck, and I found one. It was fairly steady, and I told the guy he'd be okay, not knowing if he was even able to understand me.

I kept my gun out in front of me, although I would have preferred not to use it. My only chance of that, I thought, was to talk the assailant into surrendering.

"Give up," I called out. "You're outnumbered."

Through the darkness, as my eyes got used to it, I could make out some light stands around the roof, but the lights were not on. Presumably, they were controlled by some master switch, either inside the hotel, or out there on the roof. It would have been helpful if there was a switch on the roof, and if I could find it without being shot.

I was attempting to decide what my next move should be when suddenly the rooftop was bathed in bright light.

Both of us froze when the lights went on, and our eyes locked. I watched as the assailant, who had apparently been peering over the side of the roof at the time, stared back at me and directly into the light that was behind me. I saw him clearly as he was attempting to shade his eyes so he could fire his gun.

"Put the gun down," I shouted at him. I could see him clearly and could have fired at any time. I wanted to give him the opportunity to put down his gun, but he didn't seem inclined to do so. He kept shielding his eyes, holding the gun out in front of him, as if attempting to train it on me.

"Damnit, drop the gun now!" I shouted, getting up from the crouch I had been in. I kept my gun trained on him and he began to slide along the wall in an effort to escape the lights. I could see an opening in the wall where, presumably, there was a ladder. If he attempted to go through that opening, onto the ladder, I'd have to fire.

That is, if he was even aware of the opening. If he wasn't, partially blinded as he was, he might just plunge through the opening accidently, and fall anywhere from one-to-fifteen floors.

His back was against the wall as he continued along it, and I became convinced that he was simply trying to escape the glare of the lights, and was unaware of the danger of the opening.

"Andre, look out—" I shouted. He reacted to hearing his name and began to squeeze the trigger of his gun. I had no choice but to return fire. I fired twice, and both bullets struck him in the chest just as he reached that opening in the wall. He fell through the opening, and was gone.

FORTY-TWO

"So much for your theory about the killer being a woman," Borga told me while he was being bandaged. The bullet had gone into his left shoulder, and on through without hitting anything vital. His man on the roof hadn't been as lucky. He was in intensive care, and the prognosis wasn't good. Boris was also in intensive care, but his condition was listed as stable.

Andre Dupree had been dead before he hit the ground.

"I'm not ready to give it up yet," I told Borga.

"We caught him redhanded," Borga reminded me.

"Just on Boris, and I believe that he's the one who killed Martin Leonard, but the others are a different story."

"Two murderers?" he asked.

"Two hands, two guns, one mind," I told him.

"You have to explain that," he said, standing up and, with the doctor's help, putting his shirt back on.

So I did, and he bought it.

"Reluctantly, I admit, it makes sense."

"Of course it does. Dupree could never have gotten near Belnikov, not with Vladimir and the major in the room."

"True. However, we seem to be out of bait."

"Not necessarily," I told him.

He frowned at me, then listened some more.

"I will have the equipment brought here," Borga said, looking around for a phone.

The doctor wanted him to stay overnight, but he told the doctor he would sit still for a while if he would get him a phone. The doctor agreed to the compromise.

When Borga's men arrived with the equipment, they wired me up and we were ready. I was going to have to wake her up, but that might work to my advantage.

We drove back to the hotel and went to my room. Borga and his men would set up there, since there were no other empty rooms, and we didn't want to create any kind of a disturbance by evicting anyone.

We did some testing, and when we were ready I left my room and went to hers. I had to knock a few times, which meant she was asleep. Then I had to pound on the door, which meant she was sound asleep, which said a lot for her conscience.

Finally she opened the door and squinted out at me, holding her robe tightly around her.

"Nick—" she said, but I walked past her without giving her a chance to speak further.

"It's all over," I told her. "We got Dupree, and he's talking up a storm."

She brushed her hair back from her eyes and asked, "What are you talking about?"

"You know what I'm talking about. I'm talking about you taking a husband's jealousy and using it to turn the man into a murderer. You told Andre Dupree that his wife was sleeping with Martin Leonard, and Dupree killed Leonard. You then killed Belnikov, hoping the police would think that he was killed by the same person."

"Wait a minute, wait a minute," she shouted. "Why would I kill Belnikov?"

"To keep him from defecting. He gave us the answer himself, by grabbing the red queen off his chessboard just before you marched him into the bathroom and shot him. He was telling us that his killer was a woman, a Soviet agent, and by keeping his finger over the little queen's face, he told us that the woman was a 'sleeper' agent. You were planted in the United States years ago, with a phony background, and there you stayed until they needed you."

"This is all crazy."

"I agree. You killed Belnikov, and then you went crazy, because you thought that perhaps his family was aware of the information that he was going to give to the United States."

"How would I know that those terrible people were his family?"

"You knew right from the beginning, when you first received your assignment."

"This is crazy," she said again.

"And it gets crazier. You killed Vladimir and his mother, only she tried to run, so you shot her dead and left her where she fell. You then marched Vladimir into the tub, so that his murder would look like Leonard's and Belnikov's. The police were looking for a nut who stuffed his victim's in bathtubs. Nice touch."

"Nick—"

"You must have racked your brain trying to figure out how to get to Boris, and then we up and dump him in your lap. You couldn't believe it. In fact, you knew it was too good to be true, so you decided to use Dupree again. Once you told him that his wife had slept with Boris, you just went to bed and let nature take its course."

"Where would Dupree get a gun—"

"That was easy. That's why I could never find Leonard's gun, because Dupree had it. He used it on Leonard, then kept it and tonight he used it on Boris."

"Is he dead?" she asked, perhaps a little too anxiously.

"No, Boris is in the hospital, but he's going to be all

right. You failed, and your masters aren't going to be too happy with you. You might be better off with the Swiss police."

"Don't be ridiculous. How could I possibly have killed Belnikov. I wasn't anywhere near—"

"That was clever I admit. That vase, that's what puzzled me," I admitted. "I couldn't figure out why a vase full of artificial flowers would have water in it. Then it hit me. The dampness in the rug wasn't caused by water, it was caused by melted ice. You propped that vase up with ice cubes from the ice bucket, so that when the cubes melted the vase would fall and break, attracting attention from the other room. Only, Belnikov had been dead for hours already. By the time the ice cubes melted, you were downstairs in plain sight. Perfect alibi —*you thought*."

She was silent for a few moments, just standing there with both hands in her pockets, wondering if it would be worth the effort to deny any of it.

"How'd I do?" I asked her.

With her hands still in her pockets she began to stroll around the couch, putting it between us. At that point she produced the gun from her pocket, as expected, and said, "Actually, it's damned near perfect, Nick. I'm impressed, I really am, but it's not going to do you any good to have figured it all out. You see, I don't believe that Andre Dupree is talking. In fact, he's probably dead. Am I right?"

I nodded. "You're absolutely right," I told her. "He's as dead as if you had shot him yourself."

From her other pocket she produced the silencer, the one she'd used on Belnikov first, then on Vladimir and the major. She began to apply it to the barrel of her gun, which, like Leonard's, was also a .38. I was sure close examination of all of the slugs involved would show that, although they were all .38's, they weren't all from the same gun.

"Killing me isn't going to do you any good," I assured her, opening my jacket to show her the wiring underneath.

Her eyes dropped to take in the wires, and the little microphone, and then the pounding started on the door.

"Open the door," Borga shouted from outside. "It is the police!"

She began to shake her head, as if scolding herself for being so dumb. She looked over at the door, and then back at me.

"How do you know I won't just kill you anyway, Nick?" she asked, raising the gun and pointing it at my nose.

"Because we're both pros, Nikki," I told her, stepping forward and taking the gun from her hand. "Because we're both pros."

FORTY-THREE

I had to stick around until Boris recovered enough to travel, so I got some skiing in, a little dalliance with Angel, and I even played in a couple of more matches. I didn't come anywhere near winning the whole tournament—which was won by some Italian player—but I played well enough to be satisfied with myself. I was sure even Evan Clarke wouldn't be disappointed in me. After all, he hadn't guaranteed that I would win, only that I would be able to play competitively.

Which I certainly did.

Angel still couldn't locate that telephone operator, but I told her it didn't matter anymore. Who Leonard was calling, or why, couldn't change the way things had turned out. He had simply been one of Nikki's pawns, as even I had been for a while. His murder set up the others to look like they were all done by the same nut.

I had statements to make for Borga, and we agreed that some of them should be slightly inventive, so as to make me appear as coincidently involved as possible. As promised, I wanted and took no credit for any part in solving the "bathtub murders." The officer who had been shot on the roof was credited with "capturing" Andre Dupree, and Borga himself got the credit for the arrest of Nikki Barnes.

A few days later, as I was about to leave the hotel to pick up Boris at the hospital, I received a call from Borga.

"What's up, Inspector?"

"Miss Barnes would like to see you before you leave the country," he told me. "You could easily stop in on your way to the hospital. Shall I tell her you will be here?"

"I'll be there."

When I arrived they let us use the same room I had used to talk with Boris.

"Hello, Nikki," I greeted her. She didn't look any the worse for wear, having been allowed access to her makeup daily.

"Hello, Nick. Thank you for coming."

"No problem," I assured her. "What's this all about?"

"I would like to defect," she told me.

I wasn't surprised.

"I thought you might have that in mind," I told her.

"Well, after all," she reasoned, "I've lived in the United States for more than half my life. It's more my home than anywhere else, and it's probably the only place in the world I might be safe from the Russians."

Sure. She'd be relocated, supplied with a new name and a new identity. She'd certainly last longer than she would anywhere else, but we both knew that eventually they'd get to her. I figured I'd give her a head start anyway.

Perhaps even Boris, who would also get a new name and a new life, would be the one to catch up with her.

"I'll work out the details when I get back to the States," I promised her.

"I'd really appreciate it, Nick. I only hope the Swiss can keep me out of Russian hands long enough for you to put the wheels into motion."

"I'll talk to the inspector. I'm sure he'll do all he can to cooperate."

"Thanks. Maybe we can even get together once I'm back in the States," she proposed.

"I doubt it, Nikki," I told her, honestly.

"Yes, I imagined you'd say that," she remarked. "Goodbye, Nick. I'll appreciate anything you can do for me."

"Goodbye, Nikki."

I left the room and went to Borga's office, told him about Nikki's request, and then made mine.

"You Americans," he said, shaking his head, "you accept everyone else's garbage, then wonder why your country is corrupt. Very well, I will do what I can for your Miss Barnes."

"I appreciate it, Inspector," I told him, thinking about what he'd just said.

He may have been right, too.

I extended my hand to him, and said, "Well thanks for everything. It was a genuine pleasure working with you."

He accepted my handshake, but said, "I am sorry I cannot say the same. In the future, Mr. Crane, please conduct whatever business you have, elsewhere. It would be greatly appreciated."

"I'll do my best," I promised. "I hope your man recovers."

"He is out of danger and will receive his medal shortly. He will recover very nicely, indeed."

The following day I was in Hawk's office.

"Boris Belnikov is in our medical facility," he told me, "and he is talking. He is giving us as much as he knows about Alexi Belnikov's information."

"Which is how much?"

"Not much," he admitted, "but enough to get our people off on the right track. We won't be behind the Russians for very long," he promised.

"What about Miss Barnes?"

"She is still in Swiss custody, although the Russians are trying very hard to have her transferred to theirs. I have already begun the proceedings to have her brought here. She will be supplied with a new name and new life."

I thought again about what Borga said to me just before I left Switzerland, and again felt that he may have been right.

"There is another aspect of this assignment you might be interested in," Hawk told me.

"What's that?"

"Well, it's Martin Leonard. We dug a little deeper into his background when we found out that he was once a member of the American Nazi Party."

"And?"

"It seems that when he was a member there, he was working undercover."

"You mean the guy was an agent?"

"I'm afraid so, yes. Not one of ours, but a member of a colleague agency."

"Well, what the hell was he doing in Switzerland?"

"Playing chess. It seems Mr. Leonard had hit the skids recently and was on leave of absence. It seems he was in the wrong place at the wrong time."

"Wait a minute," I said, holding up my hand. "We're going too fast. The night he died, Leonard placed a call to Washington."

"To whom?"

"I was trying to find out. I had the desk clerk there trying to find the overseas operator who placed the call, but she couldn't. Maybe he recognized someone while he was there—maybe even Nikki Barnes—and he was calling his office here in Washington."

"And then he was killed before the call could be placed."

"By a jealous husband. Damn it, if I'd only known," I snapped.

"You couldn't have known, N3, so there is no point in wishing so."

"I wonder," I said, only half aloud, "I wonder if his path and Nikki's hadn't crossed sometime in the past. Maybe his death wasn't just a tool of hers. Maybe she just saw an opportunity to kill the proverbial two birds."

"That's possible," Hawk agreed.

"Well," I said, getting up, "you can ask her when you bring her over."

"Perhaps I shall."

"You did a good job, N3," he told me, and then before I could get a swelled head he added, "As well as could be expected, under the circumstances." He wasn't done, so I waited for the rest. "A little sloppy, perhaps, but in the long run, we got most of what we were after."

Now he was done.

"Thank you, sir," I said, and started for the door. He kept on, as if I were still sitting in front of his desk.

"I've got something else lined up for you, N3. I have you on a flight tonight to—"

"Could we make that flight via Switzerland, sir?" I requested.

"Oh? Have you some unfinished business there?" he asked a little surprised.

"Actually, I do, sir," I replied, opening the door. "I've got an awful lot of explaining to do to an Angel."

DON'T MISS THE NEXT NEW
NICK CARTER SPY THRILLER

THE LAST SAMURAI

When I reached the bottom, I waited. There was a whirring noise, like a small electric motor running. It was curious. I couldn't place it. I squinted, but I couldn't see a thing.

The longer I waited, the less I liked it. I had the distinct impression coming down here was a big mistake.

I felt along the wall for a light switch, but I didn't get far. Suddenly a blunt object hit my hand. Before I could pull it back, another something, like the blunt end of a hard-swung hammer, hit the other hand and Wilhelmina dropped to the floor.

I stooped to retrieve her and got hit again, only this time I knew what it was. From the smell of leather it was a boot, and whoever he was, he wasn't the long-haired, tennis-shoe-clad kid I'd chased down here.

I needed some fighting room, so I took the blow and rolled with it, ending up face down against a pile of wet cardboard boxes.

I jumped to my feet. My hands stung from where they'd been hit, but they didn't hurt that badly that I couldn't do some damage in return. The only problem was how. By this time my eyes had adjusted to the light and I still couldn't see anything.

I sensed him moving to my right and I charged, putting up a wall of karate punches and kicks he'd be damned hard pressed to get away from. I caught him several times, once neatly on the chin because I could feel his head snap back. I moved to close in on that spot with an old-fashioned right hook when my hand hit something solid. It felt like a car door. My knuckles cracked sickeningly and a bolt of pain shot up my arm. Was that his arm? I thought.

I didn't get much time to mull this over. The next thing I knew he was using my head for a punching bag; hands, arms, elbows, all feeling like they were wrapped in cement. My knees buckled and I went down. Then he started kicking my chest and stomach, hoping to do internal damage.

He was a real pro about it, though. He knew just how far to push it. He'd stopped me pretty good, then backed off, leaving me on the floor not quite out. Then he rolled me over with his foot and triggered the spring release for my second weapon, Hugo, the pencil-thin stiletto I keep in a chamois case on my forearm. Hugo ejected and when my hand wasn't there to catch him, he skittered off across the floor.

My mystery assailant then wedged another toe under my shoulder and tried to roll me over face down, only he miscalculated. I wasn't as incapacitated as he thought. I grabbed his foot, gave it a shove, and he went tumbling into the darkness with a crash.

I dragged myself to my feet (which wasn't easy considering how I felt) and hobbled off, looking for some kind of shelter. I had no intention of fighting any more; I knew when to retreat. But I had something else in my mind. Whoever this tough guy was, he was waiting down here for one specific reason: to hurt me badly. Now I wanted to know who he was and why me.

I found a darker patch of dark which luckily turned out to be a niche of some kind. I ducked into it and leaned back against the wall to rest for a second. I knew

I didn't have much time. I had only one weapon left, Pierre, the tiny gas bomb which I keep where no personal search will ever find it, in a surgically-prepared sack near my scrotum. Pierre was my last hope.

Round and smooth, about the size of a pullet egg, Pierre was designed with a very specific talent. He was meant to be used in small confined areas where one wants to stun but not kill. He isn't much good out in the open where the gas dissipates, and he certainly isn't any good in a tiny basement where the thrower can't avoid being gassed himself. But I've found over the years that Pierre can be far more versatile if one is willing to get to know him. I unscrewed his case. There are really two bombs. In one half is the nerve gas itself, oily, smelly, and in this concentration, deadly. In the other is a propellant, a sodium chlorate compound which is highly volatile in water. I removed the plastic membrane that separates the two halves and put the one containing the nerve gas carefully on the floor. Then I looked around the corner. He was getting to his feet from where he'd fallen. I could hear him grunting. In a moment he'd come looking for me.

I chucked the chlorate crystals on the floor. My hope was there would be enough moisture there for them to react but not explosively. Sure enough, they started to sputter and smoke and a dull light filled the room.

He stood about ten feet from me, looking at the glowing chlorate in amazement. He was short, definitely Oriental, wearing a dark suit that looked two sizes too small. He had an enormous chest and back for his size, so big he strained the button of his jacket, but by far the most peculiar part of him was his head. It was shaved and the skin of it was practically translucent. Blue veins ran beneath the scalp and on both temples were large lumps of what looked like scar-tissue. He looked up and saw me staring from my niche just as the light was beginning to fail.

I dove for the floor. In the last seconds I'd seen where Wilhelmina had fallen when she'd been knocked out of my hand. If I could get her back, I could tip the scales in my direction.

I scrambled, but the beating I'd taken earlier slowed me down. He lashed out with a kick and caught me in the midsection. I curled up like a worm in a fire. From the sound of it, he'd broken a rib. He hit me a few more times; then thankfully I lost consciousness.

—From THE LAST
SAMURAI
A new Nick Carter Spy
Thriller from Ace Charter
in February